The Janeites,
The Man Who Would Be King
and
Other Stories
of Freemasonry

By Rudyard Kipling

ISBN: 978-1-63118-480-2

Esoteric Classics:
Masonic Fiction

Other Books in this Series and Related Titles

American Indian Freemasonry by A C Parker (978-1-63118-460-4)

Some Deeper Aspects of Masonic Symbolism by A E Waite (978-1-63118-461-1)

The Mysteries of Freemasonry & the Druids by various (978-1-63118-444-4)

The Smoky God or A Voyage to the Inner World by Emerson (978-1-63118-423-9)

The Two Great Pillars of Boaz and Jachin by A Mackey &c (978-1-63118-433-8)

Masonic Symbolism of King Solomon's Temple by A Mackey &c (978-1-63118-442-0)

The Regius Poem or Halliwell Manuscript by King Solomon (978-1-63118-447-5)

Psalms of Solomon by King Solomon (978-1-63118-439-0)

The Lost Keys of Freemasonry or The Secret of Hiram Abiff (978-1-63118-427-7)

Masonic Symbolism of the Apron & the Altar by various (978-1-63118-428-4)

Rosa Alchemica, The Tables of Law & The Adoration of the Magi
by William Butler Yeats (978-1-63118-421-5)

The Legend of the Holy Grail and its Connection with Templars and Freemasons
by A E Waite (978-1-63118-462-8)

Freemasonry in the Medieval or Middle Ages by various (978-1-63118-450-5)

The Kabbalah of Masonry & Related Writings by E Levi &c (978-1-63118-453-6)

Ancient Mysteries and Secret Societies by M P Hall (978-1-63118-410-9)

The Ceremony of Initiation: Analysis & Commentary (978-1-63118-473-4)

The Old Past Master by Carl H Claudy (978-1-63118-464-2)

Freemasonry and the Egyptian Mysteries by C W Leadbeater (978-1-63118-456-7)

The Master Mason's Handbook by J S M Ward (978-1-63118-474-1)

Audio Versions are also available on Audible, Amazon and Apple

Table of Contents

INTRODUCTION

The word "esoteric" can be difficult to define. Esotericism in general can be seen less as a system of beliefs and more as a category, which encompasses numerous, different systems of beliefs. It's a bit of juxtaposition, since the word "esoteric" indicates something that few people know about, while the term itself broadly covers numerous philosophies, practices, areas of study and belief systems.

In a greater sense, Esotericism acts as a storehouse for secret knowledge, which is often considered ancient (by *tradition, if not by fact)*, passed down from generation to generation, in private. At various times in history, simply possessing the knowledge of some of these subjects, was considered illegal and a jailable offence, if discovered. This usually included such general topics as Alchemy, Qabalah, Hermeticism, Occultism, Ceremonial Magic, Astrology, Divination, Rosicrucianism and so on. Collectively, these areas of study were often referred to as the esoteric sciences.

Sometimes, the outer garment of a subject isn't esoteric, while what is hidden beneath it, is. As an example, Freemasonry isn't necessarily esoteric by nature (at *least not anymore),* but certain signs, passwords and handshakes given to the candidate during their initiation, are in fact, esoteric, in the sense that they are hidden from the general public.

Today, in the twenty-first century, such topics are readily available at bookstores across the country, and numerous main-steam publishers offer beginners guides and coffee-table volumes on many of these subjects, intended for mass appeal. Books like *"The Secret"* have turned previously arcane topics into household knowledge. All that being the case, however, it isn't to say that there still aren't buried secrets to uncover, ancient wisdom being ignored and forgotten mysteries to be explored. In fact, it is often that we are only able to further our own studies by standing on the shoulders of these disappearing giants.

Lamp of Trismegistus is doing its part to help preserve humanity's esoteric history by making some of these classics available to those students who are seeking to unearth the knowledge of these ancient colossi.

So, be sure to check other titles from our *Esoteric Classics* series, as well as our *Occult Fiction*, *Theosophical Classics*, *Foundations of Freemasonry Series*, *Supernatural Fiction*, *Paranormal Research Series*, *Studies in Buddhism* and our *Christian Apocrypha Series*. You can also download the audio versions of most of these titles from Audible, Amazon or Apple, for learning on the go.

PREFACE

While some accounts list 1886 as when Rudyard Kipling became a freemason, in Kipling's autobiography, *Something of Myself,* he informs us that the year was actually 1885, when he was initiated into the masonic fraternity. It was in the city of Lahore, in what is now, modern-day Pakistan; however, the masonic initiations were performed under the auspices of an English Constitution from the British Grand Lodge. He tells us,

> "In 1885 I was made a Freemason by dispensation (*Lodge Hope and Perseverance 782 E.C.*) being under age, because the Lodge hoped for a good Secretary. They did not get him, but I helped, and got the Father to advise, on decorating the bare walls of the Masonic Hall with hangings, after the prescription of Solomon's Temple. Here I met Muslims, Sikhs, members of the Araya and Bramo Samaj, and a Jew Tyler, who was priest and butcher to his little community in the City. So yet another world opened to me which I needed."

In a private letter, Kipling further said about his lodge experience, "I was entered by a Hindu, raised by a Mohammedan, and passed by an English Master, but never rose beyond the office of Secretary." Within the York Rite, he would be advanced two years later in 1887, to the Royal Ark Mariner degree, when he joined the *Mount Ararat Mark Mariners Lodge No. 98.* He was known to visit a now-defunct military lodge, known as the *Lodge of St John the Evangelist No. 1483.* Kipling would later look back to this place and time in his life for inspiration, in both names and experiences, for some of his literary endeavors.

As Kipling mentions, he would have been required to receive dispensation from Grand Lodge, for initiation, due to only being 19 years of age, at the time. One universal requirement for admission into the fraternity is that any potential member must be of "legal age." This term has largely been reinterpreted by modern, twenty-first century masonic jurisdictions to mean 18 years or older, as this is the legal age for most other adult activities; however, at the time of Kipling's admission into the fraternity, this was almost universally understood to mean 21 years of age. As it stood, Kipling's father was already a somewhat prominent freemason, which probably was a contributing factor to why dispensation for an exception to the rule, would have been granted by Grand Lodge.

Kipling was blessed with a somewhat unique masonic upbringing, being initiated into such a cosmopolitan lodge in a foreign land. Most freemasons, both then and now, are not so lucky, and it's much more common to only meet fellow masons who follow the primary religious teachings of whatever nation or area they reside in. It is assuredly a combination of this experience, along with living through the first world war, that gave birth to the fictional lodge in these stories.

The first time Kipling incorporated his masonic knowledge into his written work, was the story, *The Man Who Would Be King*. Later, Kipling would incorporate the masonic fraternity in his full-length novel, *Kim*, as well.

With the exception of *The Man Who Would Be King*, the stories presented here largely follow mundane events in the lives of some members of the fictional masonic lodge, *Faith and Works No. 5837 E.C.* I've arranged the stories in chronological order, not of when they were published (although nearly), but based on the events in the stories. That being said, the definitive order is probably open for some interpretation, as it isn't clearly defined and must be somewhat surmised by examining context in the individual stories. As a result, other editors may disagree with the order I've chosen.

The first story, *In the Interests of the Brethren* was published in 1918, while the other 3 stories were all published in 1924. Strangely, by the time that the final 3 of these 4 stories were written and published, it had been some 35 years since he was actively involved in Craft Masonry; although, in 1909, only 20 years after being actively involved, he would go on to join the S.R.I.A., an invitational Rosicrucian body, within York Rite masonry. The S.R.I.A. was also the organization which the original *Hermetic Order of the Golden Dawn* grew out of, when it was initially formed in 1887, and perhaps it was due to the society's esoteric roots that Kipling's interest was drawn to accept that invitation for membership.

In the Interests of the Brethren subtly looks at an interesting philosophical debate, which on the surface may seem unique to freemasonry but which could be applied in a broader sense to more universal experiences. Through the background of mundane events, the visiting mason must come to terms with the fact that the Lodge is acting in a rogue fashion, not adhering to masonic protocol and ignoring the rules of their Grand Lodge, in order to offer solitude and fraternal support to wayward brothers, while simultaneously risking exposure of their meetings to any interested imposter. Should the visiting mason report their behavior to Grand Lodge, as is his responsibility and risk closing down a Lodge which may otherwise be helping actual freemasons in a serious time of need? This same theme of possible masonic cowans reappears at the beginning of the story, *A Madonna in the Trenches*.

The Janeites is the story of a group of soldiers who share the masonic bond. They have formed an unrecognized appendant body to their respective Masonic lodges. The makeshift lodge is built around their love, admiration and extensive knowledge of Jane Austen's novels, which have proven to be a source of consolation and support as they endure the horrors of trench warfare. Initiates of this shadow lodge recognize one another by references to her novels, and admission to the Austen fellowship is gained by an examination on them. Within the masonic fraternity, there are countless defunct degrees and bygone initiations, which only really still exist on paper, but which are kept living for historical sentiment as well as a segment of the masonic fraternity who like to "collect" obscure degrees, as bragging rights. It may be that Kipling's original idea for this story drew from that observation.

11

However, whatever Kipling's original intent, the story took a direction of its own. While the term "Janeite" had already technically been coined by the time Kipling used it for his title, it had only been used in an off-handed, throw-away sense. Kipling was the one who gave the word a specific definition, life and a clear path forward, giving rise to the popular movement of men exploring the literary canon of Jane Austen.

A Madonna in the Trenches is the story of a shell-shocked soldier, reliving the ghosts of his past, set between the bookends of a masonic Lodge meeting. The story intentionally invokes imagery from the *Angels of Mons* legend, a contemporary myth of the time, about British World War I soldiers, being protected and even aided in battle, by angels. These stories had been reported as fact by London newspapers but were actually an invention of fellow author Arthur Machen, and originated in his story *The Bowmen*.

The fourth tale here is *A Friend of the Family*, a story about what happens after the masonic lodge meetings have ended. Simply put, it is about a group of men sharing philosophies and swapping stories, at the refreshments table.

And finally, Kipling's most notable of the stories here, is undoubtedly *The Man Who Would Be King*. And, although it doesn't directly connect to the fictional masonic lodge mentioned in the preceding four stories, it is full of masonic references throughout.

In addition to these fictional tales, for this collection, I've also included a few of Kipling's poems, which deal with masonic themes and symbolism.

Not unlike the disappointment many men who join the masonic fraternity eventually feel, it's not difficult to see an underlying disillusion with balancing the bright-eyed wonder of a great hero's journey that lies ahead of a hopeful man, prior to being initiated, with the reality of the mundane members you actually meet on the other side of the blindfold, once the initiation is over. Kipling's stories of *Faith and Works* lodge *No.*

5837 E.C. don't highlight great thinkers or bounding adventures but instead the most average of men discussing the most average of topics. While surrounded by centuries of architecture, history and myth-making, the knight's errand is sidelined by the realities of real war and the real men who survive to recount those nightmares. These aren't the stories of great heroes on a quest, but instead, they are a snapshot into the daily lives of men who only dream of those heroes, if they dare to dream at all.

While the current stories collected here all feature freemasonry as part of the central theme, they are by no means the only time Kipling makes reference to the fraternity. In fact, he had a habit of including short and sly references in his writings, some of which would likely only get noticed by other masons.

In his story, *On the Great Wall*, Kipling references an ancient, initiatory Order, with similarities to modern Freemasonry, including penal signs:

> "We came to know each other at a ceremony in our Temple in the dark. Yes in the Cave we first met, and we were both raised to the Degree of Gryphons together. Parnesius lifted his hand toward his neck for an instant."

In a related story, *The Winged Hats*, we find a similar passage:

> "As I stopped, I saw he wore such a medal as I wear. Parnesius raised his hand to his neck. Therefore, when he could speak, I addressed him a certain question, which can only be answered in a certain manner. He answered with the necessary word; the word that belongs to the Degree of Gryphons in the science of Mithras, my God. I put my shield over him till he could stand up. He said, "What now?" I said, "At your pleasure, my brother, to stay or go?"

A much more recognizable masonic reference, often accused of being too revealing, can be found in Kipling's story, *With the Main Guard*:

> "Knee to knee!" sings out Crook, with a laugh, when the rush of our comin' into the gut shtopped, an' he was huggin' a hairy great Paythan, neither bein' able to do anything to the other, tho' both was wishful.

> "Breast to breast!" he says, as the Tyrone was pushin' us forward, closer an' closer.

> "An hand over back!" sez a sarjint that was behin'. I saw a sword lick out past Crook's ear like a snake's tongue, an' the Paythan was took in the apple av his throat like a pig at Dromean Fair.

> "Thank ye, Brother Inner-Guard." sez Crook, cool as a cucumber widout salt.

There are many other examples, as well. In Kipling's story, *Brother Square-Toes*, he makes comparisons between ceremonies within a Native American Medicine Lodge and the masonic initiations. And, in his story, *The Dog Hervey*, he utilizes the masonic method of communicating a word by lettering and halving it, between two characters. In his story, *The Wrong Thing*, Kipling interweaves masonic references, including the Royal Arch, while the characters are discussing actual stone masonry and building. Additionally, other stories make simple, passing references to the fraternity, such you'll find in his stories *Fairy-kist* and *The Bold 'Prentice*.

Kipling's poetry is certainly freemasonry told with an informal voice. Rather than symbolism at the forefront, it focuses on the comradery and brotherhood, with attention sometimes being paid to the racial and religious diversity he found in his personal lodge experience. This diversity would have been common from his perspective and it is certainly rooted in literature and tradition, but undeniably, it is idealistic and far from universal for most freemasons. Kipling frequently highlights clear attributes of the fraternity, as can be found in self-empowerment or the simplicity of being a better man, as well as the positive outcome those actions can have on the people around us.

While the eight poems collected here contain more obvious allusions to the fraternity, much like with his fiction, much of Kipling's other poetry contains sly or subtle, passing references, as well, even if the overall poem isn't centered on masonry itself.

Enjoy then, this collection delving into Rudyard Kipling's masonic writings.

IN THE INTERESTS OF THE BRETHREN

I was buying a canary in a bird shop when he first spoke to me and suggested that I should take a less highly coloured bird. "Colour's all in the feeding," said he. "Unless you know how to feed 'em, it goes. You'll excuse me, but canaries are one of my hobbies."

He passed out before I could thank him. He was a middle-aged man with gray hair and a short dark beard, rather like a Sealyham terrier in silver spectacles. For some reason his face and his voice stayed in my mind so distinctly that, months later, when I jostled against him on a platform crowded with an Angling Club going to the Thames, I recognized, turned and nodded.

"I took your advice about the canary," I said.

"Did you? Good!" he replied heartily over the rod- case on his shoulder, and was parted from me by the crowd.

*   *   *

A year ago I turned into a tobacconist's to have a badly stopped pipe cleaned out.

"Well! Well! And how did the canary do?" said the man behind the counter. We shook hands, and "What's your name?" we both asked together.

His name was Lewis Holroyd Burges, of "Burges and Son," as I might have seen above the door - but Son had been killed in Egypt. His beard was blacker and his hair whiter than it had been, and the eyes were sunk a little.

"Well! Well! To think," said he, "of one man in all these millions turning up in this curious way, when there's so many who don't turn up at all-eh?" (It was then he told me of Son Lewis's death and why the boy had been christened Lewis.) "There's not much left for middle-aged people just at present. Even one's hobbies-" he broke off for a breath. "We used to fish together. And the same with canaries! We used to breed 'em for colour - deep orange was our specialty. That's why I spoke to you, if you remember, but I've sold all my birds. Well! Well! And now we must locate your trouble."

He bent over my erring pipe and dealt with it skilfully as a surgeon. A soldier came in, said something in an undertone, received a reply, and went out.

"Many of my clients are soldiers nowadays, and a number of 'em belong to the Craft," said Mr. Burges. "It breaks my heart to give them the tobaccos they ask for. On the other hand, not one man in five thousand has a tobacco palate. Preference, yes. Palate, no. Here's your pipe. It deserves better treatment than it's had. There's a procedure, a ritual, in all things. Any time you're passing by again, I assure you, you will be most welcome. I've one or two odds and ends that may interest you."

I left the shop with the rarest of all feelings on me - that sensation which is only youth's right - that I had made a friend. A little distance from the door I was accosted by a wounded man who asked for "Burges's." The place seemed to be known in the neighbourhood.

I found my way to it again, and often after that, but it was not till my third visit that I discovered Mr. Burges held a half interest in Ackman and Permit's, the great cigar importers, which had come to him through an uncle whose children now lived almost in the Cromwell Road, and said that uncle had been on the Stock Exchange.

"I'm a shopkeeper by instinct," said Mr. Burges. "I like the ritual of handling things. The shop has always done us well. I like to do well by the shop."

It had been established by his grandfather in 1827, but the fittings and appointments were at least half a century older. The brown and red tobacco and snuff jars, with Crowns, Garters, and names of forgotten mixtures in gold leaf, the polished "Oronoque" tobacco barrels on which favoured customers sat, the cherry-black mahogany counter, the delicately moulded shelves, the reeded cigar- cabinets, the German-silver mounted scales, and the Dutch brass roll and cake-cutter were things to covet.

"They aren't so bad," he admitted. "That large Bristol jar hasn't any duplicate to my knowledge. Those eight snuff-jars on the third shelf - they're Dollin's ware; he used to work for Wimble in Seventeen-Forty - they're absolutely unique. Is there anyone in the trade now could tell you what 'Romano's Hollande' was? Or 'Scholten's,' or 'John's Lane'? Here's a snuff-mull of George the First's time; and here's a Louis Quinze - what am I talking of? Treize, Treize, of course - grater for making bran- snuff. They were regular tools of the shop in my grandfather's day. And who on earth to leave 'em to outside the British Museum now, I can't think!"

His pipes - I wish this were a tale for virtuosi - his amazing pipes were kept in the parlour, and this gave me the privilege of making his wife's acquaintance. One morning, as I was looking covetously at a jacaranda-wood "cigarro" - not cigar - cabinet with silver lock-plates and drawer-knobs of Spanish work, a wounded Canadian came into the shop and disturbed our happy little committee.

"Say," he began loudly, "are you the right place?"

"Who sent you?" Mr. Burges demanded.

"A man from Messines. But that ain't the point!

I've got no certificates, nor papers-nothin', you understand. I left Lodge owin' 'em seventeen dollars back dues. But this man at Messines told me it wouldn't make any odds here."

"It doesn't," said Mr. Burges. "We meet tonight at 7 p.m."

The man's face fell a yard. "Hell!" said he. "But I'm in hospital - I can't get leave."

"And Tuesdays and Fridays at 3 p.m.," Mr. Burges added promptly. "You'll have to be proved, of course."

"Guess I can get by that, all right," was the cheery reply. "Toosday, then."

He limped off, beaming.

"Who might that be?" I asked.

"I don't know any more than you do - except he must be a Brother. London's full of Masons now. Well! Well! We must all do what we can these days. If you come to tea this evening, I'll take you on to Lodge afterward. It's a Lodge of Instruction."

"Delighted. Which is your Lodge?" I said, for up till then he had not given me its name.

"'Faith and Works 5837' - the third Saturday of every month. Our Lodge of Instruction meets nominally every Thursday, but we sit oftener than that now because there are so many Visiting Brethren in town." Here another customer entered, and I went away much interested in the range of Brother Burges's hobbies.

At tea-time he was dressed as for Church, and with gold pince-nez in lieu of the silver spectacles. I blessed my stars that I had thought to change into decent clothes.

"Yes, we owe that much to the Craft," he assented. "All Ritual is fortifying. Ritual's a natural necessity for mankind. The more things are upset, the more they fly to it. I abhor slovenly Ritual anywhere. By the way, would you mind assisting at the examinations, if there are many Visiting Brothers tonight? You'll find some of 'em very rusty but - it's the Spirit, not the Letter, that giveth life. The question of Visiting Brethren is an important one. There are so many of them in London now, you see; and so few places where they can meet."

"You dear thing!" said Mrs. Burges, and handed him his locked and initialed apron-case.

"Our Lodge is only just round the corner," he went on. "You mustn't be too critical of our appurtenances. The place was a garage once."

As far as I could make out in the humiliating darkness, we wandered up a mews and into a courtyard. Mr. Burges piloted me, murmuring apologies for everything in advance.

"You mustn't expect-" he was still saying when we stumbled up a porch and entered a carefully decorated anteroom hung round with masonic prints. I noticed Peter Gilkes and Barton Wilson, fathers of "Emulation" working, in the place of honour; Kneller's Christopher Wren; Dunkerley, with his own Fitz- George book-plate below and the bend sinister on the Royal Arms; Hogarth's caricature of Wilkes, also his disreputable "Night," and a beautifully framed set of Grand Masters, from Anthony Sayer down.

"Are these another of your hobbies?" I asked.

"Not this time," Mr. Burges smiled. "We have to thank Brother Lemming for them." He introduced me to the senior partner of Lemming and Orton, whose dirty little shop is hard to find, but whose words and cheques in the matter of prints are widely circulated.

"The frames are the best part of said Brother Lemming after my compliments. "There are some more in the Lodge Room. Come and look. We've got the big Desaguliers there that neatly went to Iowa."

I had never seen a Lodge Room better fitted. From mosaicked floor to appropriate ceiling, from curtain to pillar, implements to seats, seats to lights, and little carved music-loft at one end, every detail was perfect in particular kind and general design. I said what I thought many times over.

"I told you I was a Ritualist," said Mr.Burges. "Look at those carved corn-sheaves and grapes on the back of these Warden's chairs. That's the old tradition-before Masonic furnishers spoiled it. I picked up that pair in Stepney ten years ago-the same time I got the gavel." It was of old, yellowed ivory, cut all in one piece out of some tremendous tusk. "That came from the Gold Coast," he said. "It belonged to a Military Lodge there in 1794. You can see the inscription."

"If it's a fair question-" I began, "how much---"

"It stood us," said Brother Lemming, his thumbs in his waistcoat pockets, "an appreciable sum of money when we built it in 1906, even with what Brother Anstruther - he was our contractor - cheated himself out of. By the way, that block there is pure Carrara, he tells me. I don't understand marbles myself. Since the war I expect we've put in - oh, quite another little sum. Now we'll go to the examination- room and take on the Brethren."

He led me back, not to the anteroom, but a convenient chamber flanked with what looked like confessional-boxes (I found out later that was what they had been when first picked up for a song near Oswestry). A few men in uniform were waiting at the far end. "That's only the head of the procession. The rest are in the anteroom," said an officer of the Lodge.

Brother Burges assigned me my discreet box, saying: "Don't be surprised. They come all shapes."

"Shapes" was not a bad description, for my first penitent was all head-bandages - escaped from an Officers' Hospital, Pentonville way. He asked me in profane Scots how I expected a man with only six teeth and half a lower lip to speak to any purpose, and we compromised on signs. The next - a New Zealander from Taranaki - reversed the process, for he was one-armed, and that in a sling. I mistrusted an enormous Sergeant-Major of Heavy Artillery, who struck me as much too glib, so I sent him on to Brother Lemming in the next box, who discovered he was a Past District Grand Officer. My last man nearly broke me down altogether. Everything seemed to have gone from him.

"I don't blame yer," he gulped at last. "I wouldn't pass my own self on my answers, but I give yer my word that so far as I've had any religion, it's been all the religion I've had. For God's sake, let me sit in Lodge again, Brother."

When the examinations were ended, a Lodge Officer came round with our aprons - no tinsel or silver-gilt confections, but heavily-corded silk with tassels and - where a man could prove he was entitled to them - levels, of decent plate. Someone in front of me tightened the belt on a stiffly silent person in civil clothes with discharge badge. "'Strewth! This is comfort again," I heard him say. The companion nodded. The man went on suddenly: "Here! What're you doing? Leave off! You promised not to! Chuck it!" and dabbed at his companion's streaming eyes.

"Let him leak," said an Australian signaler. "Can't you see how happy the beggar is?"

It appeared that the silent Brother was a "shell- shocker" whom Brother Lemming had passed, on the guarantee of his friend and - what moved Lemming more - the threat that, were he refused, he would have fits from pure disappointment. So the "shocker" wept happily and silently among Brethren evidently accustomed to these displays.

We fell in, two by two, according to tradition, fifty of us at least, and we played into Lodge by the harmonium, which I discovered was in reality an organ of repute. It took time to settle us down, for ten or twelve were cripples and had to be helped into long and easy-chairs. I sat between a one-footed R.A.M.C. Corporal and a Captain of Territorials, who, he told me, had "had a brawl" with a bomb, which had bent him in two directions. "But that's first-class Bach the organist is giving us now," he said delightedly. "I'd like to know him. I used to be a piano-thumper of sorts."

"I'll introduce you after Lodge," said one of the regular Brethren behind us - a fat, torpedo-bearded man, who turned out to be the local Doctor. "After all, there's nobody to touch Bach, is there?" Those two plunged at once into musical talk, which to outsiders is as fascinating as trigonometry.

"Now a Lodge of Instruction is mainly a parade- ground for Ritual. It cannot initiate or confer degrees, but is limited to rehearsals and lectures. Worshipful Brother Burges, resplendent in Solomon's Chair (I found out later where that, too, had been picked up), briefly told the Visiting Brethren how welcome they were and always would be, and asked them to vote what ceremony should be rendered for their instruction.

When the decision was announced he wanted to know whether any Visiting Brothers would take the duties of any Lodge Officers. They protested bashfully that they were too rusty. "The very reason why," said Brother Burges, while the organ Bached softly. My musical Captain sighed and wriggled in his chair.

"One moment, Worshipful Sir." The fat Doctor rose. "We have here a musician for whom place and opportunity are needed. Only," he went on colloquially, "those organ-loft steps are a bit steep."

"How much," said Brother Burges, with the solemnity of an initiation, "does our Brother weigh?"

"Very little over eight stone," said the Brother. "'Weighed this mornin', sir."

The Past District Grand Officer, who was also Battery Sergeant-Major, waddled across, lifted the slight weight in his arms and bore it to the loft, where, the regular organist pumping, it played joyously as a soul caught up to Heaven by surprise.

When the visitors had been coaxed to supply the necessary officers, a ceremony was rehearsed. Brother Burges forbade the regular members to prompt. The visitors had to work entirely by themselves, but, on the Battery Sergeant-Major taking a hand, he was ruled out as of too exalted rank. They floundered badly after that support was withdrawn.

The one-footed R.A.M.C. on my right chuckled.

"D'you like it?" said the Doctor to him.

"Do I? It's Heaven to me, sittin' in Lodge again. It's all comin' back now, watching their mistakes. I haven't much religion, but all I had I learned in Lodge." Recognizing me, he flushed a little as one does when one says a thing twice over in another's hearing. "Yes, 'veiled in all'gory and illustrated by symbols' - the Fatherhood of God, an' the Brotherhood of Man, an' what more in Hell do you want? ... Look at 'em!" He broke off, giggling. "See! See! They've tied the whole thing into knots. I could ha' done better myself - my one foot in France. Yes, I should think they ought to do it over again!"

The new organist covered the little confusion that had arisen with what sounded like the wings of angels.

When the amateurs, rather red and hot, had finished, they demanded an exhibition-working of their bungled ceremony by Regular Brethren of the Lodge. Then I realized for the first time what word-and-gesture-perfect Ritual can be brought to mean. We all applauded, the one-footed Corporal most of all. It was a revelation.

"We are rather proud of our working, and this is an audience worth playing up to," the Doctor said.

Next the Master delivered a little lecture on the meanings of some pictured symbols and diagrams. His theme was a well-worn one, but his deep holding voice made it fresh.

"Marvellous how these old copybook headings persist," the Doctor said.

"That's all right!" the one-footed man spoke cautiously out of the side of his mouth like a boy in form. "But they're the kind of copybook headin's we shall find burnin' round our bunk in Hell. Believe me-ee! I've broke enough of 'em to know Now, h'sh!" He leaned forward, drinking it all in.

Presently Brother Burges touched on a point which had given rise to some diversity of Ritual. He asked for information. "Well, in Jamaica, Worshipful Sir," a Visiting Brother began, and explained how they worked that detail in his parts. Another and another joined in from different quarters of the Lodge (and the world), and when they were warmed the Doctor sidled softly round the walls and, over our shoulders, passed us cigarettes.

"A shocking innovation," he said as he returned to the captain-musician's vacant seat on my left. "But men can't really talk without tobacco, and we're only a Lodge of Instruction."

"An' I've learned more in one evenin' here than ten years.' The one-footed man turned round for an instant from a dark sour-looking Yeoman in spurs who was laying down the law on Dutch Ritual. The blue haze and the talk increased, while the organ from the loft blessed us all.

"But this is delightful," said I to the Doctor. "How did it all happen?"

"Brother Burges started it. He used to talk to the men who dropped into his shop when the war began. He told us sleepy old chaps in Lodge that what men wanted more than anything else was Lodges where they could sit - just sit and be happy like we are now. He was right, too. He generally is. We're learning things in the War. A man's lodge means move to him than people imagine. As our friend on your right said just now, very often Masonry's the only practical creed we've ever listened to since we were children. Platitudes or no platitudes, it squares with what everybody knows ought to be done." He sighed. "And if this war hasn't brought home the Brotherhood of Man to us all, I'm a - a Hun!"

"How did you get your visitors?" I went on.

"Oh I told a few fellows in hospital near here, at Burges's suggestion, that we had a Lodge of Instruction and they'd be welcome. And they came, And they told their friends. And they came! That was two years ago - and now we've Lodge of Instruction two nights a week, and a matinee nearly every Tuesday and Friday for the men who can't get evening-leave. Yes, it's all very curious. I'd no notion what the Craft meant - and means - till this war."

"Nor I till this evening," I replied.

"Yet it's quite natural if you think. Here's London - all England - packed with the Craft from all over the world, and nowhere for them to go. Why, our weekly visiting attendance for the last four months averaged just under a hundred and forty. Divide by four - call it thirty-five Visiting Brethren a time. Our record's seventy-one, but we have packed in as many as eighty- four at banquets. You can see for yourself what a potty little hole we are!"

"Banquets, too!" I cried. "It must cost like all sin. May the Visiting Brethren-"

The Doctor laughed. "No, a Visiting Brother may not."

"But when a man has had an evening like this he wants to-"

"That's what they all say. That makes our difficulty. They do exactly what you were going to suggest, and they're offended if we don't take it."

"Don't you?" I asked.

"My dear man - what does it come to? They can't all stay to banquet. Say one hundred suppers a week - fifteen quid - sixty a month - seven hundred and twenty a year. How much are Lemming and Orton worth? And Ellis and McKnight - that long thin man over yonder - the provision dealers? How much d'you suppose could Burges write a cheque for and not feel? 'Tisn't as if he had to save for any one now. And the same with Anstruther. I assure you we have no scruple in calling on the Visiting Brethren when we want anything. We couldn't do the work otherwise. Have you noticed how the Lodge is kept - brasswork, jewels, furniture and so on?"

"I have indeed," I said. "It's like a ship. You could eat your dinner off the floor."

"Well, come here on a by-day and you'll often find half a dozen Brethren, with eight legs between 'em, polishing and ronuking and sweeping everything they can get at. I cured a shell-shocker this spring by giving him our jewels to look after. He pretty well polished the numbers off them, but - it kept him from fighting the Huns in his sleep. And when we need Masters to take our duties - two matinees a week is rather a tax - we've the choice of P.M.'s from all over the world. The Dominions are much keener on Ritual than an average English Lodge. Besides that- Oh, we're going to adjourn. Listen to the greetings. They'll be interesting."

The crack of the great gavel brought us to our feet, after some surging and plunging among the cripples. Then the Battery Sergeant-Major, in a trained voice, delivered hearty and fraternal greetings to "Faith and Works" from his tropical District and Lodge. The others followed, without order, in every tone between a grunt and a squeak. I heard "Hauraki," "Inyanga-Umbezi," "Aloha," "Southern Lights" (from somewhere Puntas Arenas way), "Lodge of Rough Ashlars" (and that Newfoundland Brother looked it), two or three "Stars" of something or other, half a dozen cardinal virtues, variously arranged, hailing from Klondyke to Kalgoorlie, one Military Lodge on one of the fronts, thrown in with a severe Scots burr by my friend of the head-bandages, and the rest as mixed as the Empire itself. Just at the end there was a little stir. The silent Brother had begun to make noises; his companion tried to soothe him.

"Let him be! Let him be!" the Doctor called professionally. The man jerked and mouthed, and at last mumbled something unintelligible even to his friend, but a small, dark P.M. pushed forward importantly.

"It is all right," he said. "He wants to say," he spat out some yard-long Welsh name, adding, "That means Pembroke Docks, Worshipful Sir. We haf good Masons in Wales, too." The silent man nodded approval.

"Yes," said the Doctor, quite unmoved. "It happens that way sometimes. *Hespere panta fereis,* isn't it? The Star brings 'em all home. I must get a note of that fellow's case after Lodge. I know you don't care for music," he went on, "but I'm afraid you'll have to put up with a little more.

28

It's a paraphrase from Micah. Our organist arranged it. We sing it antiphonally, as a sort of dismissal."

Even I could appreciate what followed. The singing seemed confined to half a dozen trained voices answering each other till the last line, when the full Lodge came in. I give it as I heard it:

> "We have showed thee, O Man,
>> What is good.
> What doth the Lord require of us?
> Or Consciences' self desire of us?
>> But to do justly
>> And to love mercy
> And to walk humbly with our God
>> As every Mason should."

Then we were played and sung out to the quaint tune of the "Entered Apprentices' Song." I noticed that the regular Brethren of the Lodge did not begin to take off their regalia till the lines:

> "Great Kings, Dukes and Lords
> Have laid down their swords."

They moved into the anteroom, now set for the banquet, on the verse:

> "Antiquity's pride
> We have on our side,
> Which maketh men just in their station."

The Brother (a big-boned clergyman) that I found myself next to at table told me the custom was "a fond thing vainly invented" on the strength of some old legend. He laid down that Masonry should be regarded as an "intellectual abstraction." An Officer of Engineers disagreed with him, and told us how in Flanders, a year before, some ten or twelve Brethren held Lodge in what was left of a Church. Save for the Emblems of Mortality and plenty of rough ashlars, there was no furniture.

"I warrant you weren't a bit the worse for that," said the clergyman. "The idea should be enough without trappings."

"But it wasn't," said the other. "We took a lot of trouble to make our regalia out of camouflage-stuff that we'd pinched, and we manufactured our jewels from old metal. I've got the set now. It kept us happy for weeks."

"Ye were absolutely irregular an'unauthorised. Whaur was your warrant?" said the Brother from the Military Lodge. "Grand Lodge ought to take steps against---"

"If Grand Lodge had any sense," a private three places up our table broke in, "it 'ud warrant travelling Lodges at the front and attach first-class lecturers to 'em."

"Wad ye confer degrees promiscuously?" said the scandalised Scot.

"Every time a man asked, of course. You'd have half the Army in."

The speaker played with the idea for a little while, and proved that on the lowest scale of fees Grand Lodge would get huge revenues.

"I believe," said the Engineer Officer thoughtfully, "I could design a complete travelling Lodge outfit under forty pounds weight."

"Ye're wrong. I'll prove it. We've tried ourselves," said the Military Lodge man; and they went at it together across the table, each with his own note- book.

The "banquet" was simplicity itself. Many of us ate in haste so as to get back to barracks or hospitals, but now and again a Brother came in from the outer darkness to fill a chair and empty a plate. These were Brethren who had been there before and needed no examination.

One man lurched in - helmet, Flanders mud, accoutrements and all - fresh from the leave-train.

"Got two hours to wait for my train," he explained. "I remembered your night, though. My God, this is good!"

"What is your train and from which station?" said the clergyman, precisely. "Very well. What will you have to eat?"

"Anything. Everything. I've thrown up a month's feed off Folkestone."

He stoked himself for ten minutes without a word. Then, without a word, his face fell forward. The clergyman had him by one already limp arm and steered him to a couch, where he dropped and snored. No one took the trouble to turn round.

"Is that usual too?" I asked.

"Why not?" said the clergyman. "I'm on duty tonight to wake them for their trains. They do not respect the cloth on those occasions." He turned his broad back on me and continued his discussion with a Brother from Aberdeen by way of Mitylene where, in the intervals of mine-sweeping, he had evolved a complete theory of the Revelations of St. John the Divine in the Island of Patmos.

I fell into the hands of a Sergeant-Instructor of Machine Guns - by profession a designer of ladies' dresses. He told me that Englishwomen as a class "lose on their corsets what they make on their clothes," and that "Satan himself can't save a woman who wears thirty-shilling corsets, under a thirty- guinea costume." Here, to my grief, he was buttonholed by an earnest Lieutenant of his own branch, and became a Sergeant again all in one click.

I drifted back and forth, studying the prints on the walls and the Masonic collections in the cases, while I listened to the inconceivable talk all round me. Little by little the company thinned, till at last there were only a dozen or so of us left. We gathered at the end of a table by the fire, the night-bird from Flanders trumpeting lustily into the hollow of his helmet, which someone bad tipped over his face.

"And how did it go with you?" said the Doctor.

"It was like a new world," I answered.

"That's what it is really." Brother Burges returned the gold pince-nez to their case and reshipped his silver spectacles. "Or that's what it might be made with a little trouble. When I think of the possibilities of he Craft at this juncture I wonder--" He stared into the fire.

"I wonder, too," said the Sergeant-Major slowly, "but - on the whole - I'm inclined to agree with you. We could do much with Masonry."

"As an aid - as an aid - not as a substitute for Religion," the clergyman snapped.

"Oh, Lord! Can't we give Religion a rest for a bit," the Doctor muttered. "It hasn't done so - I beg your pardon all round."

The clergyman was bristling. "Kamerad!" the wise Sergeant-Major went on, both hands up. "Certainly not as a substitute for a creed, but as an average plan of life. What I've seen at the front makes me sure of it."

Brother Burges came out of his muse. "There ought to be dozen - twenty - other Lodges in London every night; conferring degrees too, as well as instruction, Why shouldn't the young men join? They practice what we're always preaching. Well! Well! We must all do what we can. What's the use of old Masons if they can't give a little help along their own lines?"

"Exactly," said the Sergeant-Major, turning on the Doctor. "And what's the darn use of a Brother if he isn't allowed to help?"

"Have it your own way then," said the Doctor testily. He had evidently been approached before. He took something the Sergeant-Major handed to him and pocketed it with a nod. "I was wrong," he said to me, "when I boasted of our independence. They get round us sometimes. This," he slapped his pocket, "will give a banquet on Tuesday. We don't usually feed at matinees. It will be a surprise. By the way, try another sandwich. The ham are best." He pushed me a plate.

"They are," I said. "I've only had five or six. I've been looking for them."

"Glad you like them," said Brother Lemming. "Fed him myself, cured him myself - at my little place in Berkshire. His name was Charlemagne. By the way, Doc, am I to keep another one for next month?"

"Of course," said the Doctor, with his mouth full. "A little fatter than this chap, please. And don't forget your promise about the pickled nasturtiums. They're appreciated." Brother Lemming nodded above the pipe he had lit as we began a second supper. Suddenly the clergyman, after a glance at the clock, scooped up half a dozen sandwiches from under my nose, put them into an oiled-paper bag, and advanced cautiously towards the sleeper on the couch.

"They wake rough sometimes," said the Doctor. "Nerves, y'know." The clergyman tiptoed directly behind the man's head, and at arm's length rapped on the dome of the helmet. The man woke in one vivid streak, as the clergyman stepped back, and grabbed for a rifle that was not there.

"You've barely half an hour to catch your train." The clergyman passed him the sandwiches. "Come along."

"You're uncommonly kind and I'm very grateful," said the man, wriggling into his stiff straps. He followed his guide into the darkness after saluting.

"Who's that?" said Lemming.

"Can't say," the Doctor returned indifferently. "He's been here before. He's evidently a P.M. of sorts."

"Well! Well!" said Brother Burges, whose eyelids were drooping. "We must all do what we can. Isn't it almost time to lock up?"

"I wonder," said I, as we helped each other into our coats, "what would happen if Grand Lodge knew about all this."

"About what?" Lemming turned on me quickly.

"A Lodge of Instruction open three nights and two afternoons a week - and running a lodging-house as well. It's all very nice, but it doesn't strike me somehow as regulation."

"The point hasn't been raised yet," said Lemming. "We'll settle it after the war. Meantime we shall go on."

"There ought to be scores of them," Brother Burges repeated as we went out of the door. "All London's full of the Craft, and no places for them to meet in. Think of the possibilities of it! Think what could have been done by Masonry through Masonry for all the world. I hope I'm not censorious, but it sometimes crosses my mind that Grand Lodge may have thrown away its chance in the war almost as much as the Church has."

"Lucky for you Brother Tamworth is taking that chap to King's Cross," said Brother Lemming, "or he'd be down your throat. What really troubles Tamworth is our legal position under Masonic Law. I think he'll inform on us one of these days. Well, good night all." The Doctor and Lemming turned off together.

"Yes," said Brother Burges, slipping his arm into mine. "Almost as much as the Church has. But perhaps I'm too much of a Ritualist."

I said nothing. I was speculating how soon I could steal a march on Brother Tamworth and inform against "Faith and Works No. 5837 E. C."

THE JANEITES

Jane lies in Winchester—blessed be her shade!
Praise the Lord for making her, and her for all she made!
And while the stones of Winchester, or Milsom Street, remain,
Glory, love, and honour unto England's Jane!

In the Lodge of Instruction attached to 'Faith and Works No. 5837 E.C.,' which has already been described, Saturday afternoon was appointed for the weekly clean-up, when all visiting Brethren were welcome to help under the direction of the Lodge Officer of the day: their reward was light refreshment and the meeting of companions.

This particular afternoon—in the autumn of '20—Brother Burges, P.M., was on duty and, finding a strong shift present, took advantage of it to strip and dust all hangings and curtains, to go over every inch of the Pavement—which was stone, not floorcloth—by hand; and to polish the Columns, Jewels, Working outfit and organ. I was given to clean some Officers' Jewels—beautiful bits of old Georgian silver-work humanized by generations of elbow-grease—and retired to the organ-loft; for the floor was like the quarterdeck of a battleship on the eve of a ball. Half-a-dozen brethren had already made the Pavement as glassy as the aisle of Greenwich Chapel; the brazen chapiters winked like pure gold at the flashing Marks on the Chairs; and a morose one-legged brother was attending to the Emblems of Mortality with, I think, rouge.

'They ought,' he volunteered to Brother Burges as we passed, 'to be betwixt the colour of ripe apricots an' a half-smoked meerschaum. That's how we kept 'em in my Mother-Lodge—a treat to look at.'

'I've never seen spit-and-polish to touch this,' I said.

'Wait till you see the organ,' Brother Burges replied. 'You could shave in it when they've done. Brother Anthony's in charge up there—

35

the taxi-owner you met here last month. I don't think you've come across Brother Humberstall, have you?'

'I don't remember—' I began.

'You wouldn't have forgotten him if you had. He's a hairdresser now, somewhere at the back of Ebury Street. Was Garrison Artillery. Blown up twice.'

'Does he show it?' I asked at the foot of the organ-loft stairs.

'No-o. Not much more than Lazarus did, I expect.' Brother Burges fled off to set someone else to a job.

Brother Anthony, small, dark, and humpbacked, was hissing groom-fashion while he treated the rich acacia-wood panels of the Lodge organ with some sacred, secret composition of his own. Under his guidance Humberstall, an enormous, flat-faced man, carrying the shoulders, ribs, and loins of the old Mark '14 Royal Garrison Artillery, and the eyes of a bewildered retriever, rubbed the stuff in. I sat down to my task on the organ-bench, whose purple velvet cushion was being vacuum-cleaned on the floor below.

'Now,' said Anthony, after five minutes vigorous work on the part of Humberstall. '*Now* we're gettin' somethin' worth lookin' at! Take it easy, an' go on with what you was tellin' me about that Macklin man.'

'I—I 'adn't anything against 'im,' said Humberstall, 'excep' he'd been a toff by birth; but that never showed till he was bosko absoluto. Mere bein' drunk on'y made a common 'ound of 'im. But when bosko, it all came out. Otherwise, he showed me my duties as mess-waiter very well on the 'ole.'

36

'Yes, yes. But what in 'ell made you go *back* to your Circus? The Board gave you down-an'-out fair enough, you said, after the dump went up at Eatables?'

'Board or no Board, *I* 'adn't the nerve to stay at 'ome—not with Mother chuckin' 'erself round all three rooms like a rabbit every time the Gothas tried to get Victoria; an' sister writin' me aunts four pages about it next day. Not for *me*, thank you! till the war was over. So I slid out with a draft—they wasn't particular in '17, so long as the tally was correct— and I joined up again with our Circus somewhere at the back of Lar Pug Noy, I think it was.' Humberstall paused for some seconds and his brow wrinkled. 'Then I—I went sick, or somethin' or other, they told me; but I know *when* I reported for duty, our Battery Sergeant-Major says that I wasn't expected back, an'—an', one thing leadin' to another—to cut a long story short—I went up before our Major—Major—I shall forget my own name next-Major——'

'Never mind,' Anthony interrupted. 'Go on! It'll come back in talk!'

"Alf a mo'. 'Twas on the tip o' my tongue then.'

Humberstall dropped the polishing-cloth and knitted his brows again in most profound thought. Anthony turned to me and suddenly launched into a sprightly tale of his taxi's collision with a Marble Arch refuge on a greasy day after a three-yard skid.

"Much damage?' I asked.

'Oh no! Ev'ry bolt an' screw an' nut on the chassis strained; *but* nothing carried away, you understand me, an' not a scratch on the body. You'd never 'ave guessed a thing wrong till you took 'er in hand. It was a *wop* too: 'ead-on—like this!' And he slapped his tactful little forehead to show what a knock it had been.

'Did your Major dish you up much?' he went on over his shoulder to Humberstall, who came out of his abstraction with a slow heave.

'We-ell! He told me I wasn't expected back either; an' he said 'e couldn't 'ang up the 'ole Circus till I'd rejoined; an' he said that my ten-inch Skoda which I'd been Number Three of, before the dump went up at Eatables, had 'er full crowd. But, 'e said, as soon as a casualty occurred he'd remember me. "Meantime," says he, "I particularly want you for actin' mess-waiter."

"'Beggin' your pardon, sir," I says perfectly respectful; "but I didn't exactly come back for *that*, sir."

"'Beggin' *your* pardon, 'Umberstall," says 'e, "but I 'appen to command the Circus! Now, you're a sharp-witted man," he says; "an' what we've suffered from fool-waiters in Mess 'as been somethin' cruel. You'll take on, from now—under instruction to Macklin 'ere." So this man, Macklin, that I was tellin' you about, showed me my duties . . . . 'Ammick! I've got it! 'Ammick was our Major, an' Mosse was Captain!' Humberstall celebrated his recapture of the name by labouring at the organ-panel on his knee.

'Look out! You'll smash it,' Anthony protested.

'Sorry! Mother's often told me I didn't know my strength. Now, here's a curious thing. This Major of ours—it's ail comin' back to me—was a high-up divorce-court lawyer; an' Mosse, our Captain, was Number One o' Mosses Private Detective Agency. You've heard of it? 'Wives watched while you wait, an' so on. Well, these two 'ad been registerin' together, so to speak, in the Civil line for years on end, but hadn't ever met till the War. Consequently, at Mess their talk was mostly about famous cases they'd been mixed up in. 'Ammick told the Law-courts' end o' the business, an' all what had been left out of the pleadin's; an' Mosse 'ad the actual facts concernin' the errin' parties—in hotels an' so on. I've heard better talk in our Mess than ever before or since. It comes o' the Gunners bein' a scientific corps.'

'That be damned!' said Anthony. 'If anythin' 'appens to 'em they've got it all down in a book. There's no book when your lorry dies on you in the 'Oly Land. *That's* brains.'

'Well, *then*,' Humberstall continued, 'come on this secret society business that I started tellin' you about. When those two—'Ammick an' Mosse—'ad finished about their matrimonial relations—and, mind you, they weren't radishes—they seldom or ever repeated—they'd begin, as often as not, on this Secret Society woman I was tellin' you of—this Jane. She was the only woman I ever 'eard 'em say a good word for. 'Cordin' to them Jane was a none-such. *I* didn't know then she was a Society. 'Fact is, I only 'ung out 'arf an ear in their direction at first, on account of bein' under instruction for mess-duty to this Macklin man. What drew *my* attention to her was a new Lieutenant joinin' up. We called 'im "Gander" on account of his profeel, which was the identical bird. 'E'd been a nactuary—workin' out 'ow long civilians 'ad to live. Neither 'Ammick nor Mosse wasted words on 'im at Mess. They went on talking as usual, an' in due time, as usual, they got back to Jane. Gander cocks one of his big chilblainy ears an' cracks his cold finger joints. "By God! Jane?" says 'e. "Yes, Jane," says 'Ammick pretty short an' senior. "Praise 'Eaven!" says Gander. "It was 'Bubbly' where I've come from down the line." (Some damn revue or other, I expect.) Well, neither 'Ammick nor Mosse was easy-mouthed, or for that matter mealy-mouthed; but no sooner 'ad Gander passed that remark than they both shook 'ands with the young squirt across the table an' called for the port back again. It *was* a password, all right! Then they went at it about Jane—all three, regardless of rank. That made me listen. Presently, I 'eard 'Ammick say——'

"Arf a mo',' Anthony cut in. 'But what was *you* doin' in Mess?'

'Me an' Macklin was refixin' the sand-bag screens to the dug-out passage in case o' gas. We never knew when we'd cop it in the 'Eavies, don't you see? But we knew we 'ad been looked for for some time, an' it might come any minute. But, as I was sayin', 'Ammick says what a pity 'twas Jane 'ad died barren. "I deny that," says Mosse. "I maintain she was fruitful in the 'ighest sense o' the word." An' Mosse knew about such things, too. "I'm inclined to agree with 'Ammick," says young Gander. "Any'ow, she's left no direct an' lawful prog'ny." I remember every word they said, on account o' what 'appened subsequently. I 'adn't noticed Macklin much, or I'd ha' seen he was bosko absoluto. Then *'e* cut in, leanin' over a packin'-case with a face on 'im like a dead mackerel in the dark. "Pa-hardon me, gents," Macklin says, "but this is a matter on which I *do* 'appen to be moderately well-informed. She *did* leave lawful issue in the shape o' one son; an' 'is name was 'Enery James."

"'By what sire? Prove it," says Gander, before 'is senior officers could get in a word.

"'I will," says Macklin, surgin' on 'is two thumbs. *An'*, mark you, none of 'em spoke! I forget whom he said was the sire of this 'Enery James-man; but 'e delivered 'em a lecture on this Jane-woman for more than a quarter of an hour. I know the exact time, because my old Skoda was on duty at ten-minute intervals reachin' after some Jerry formin'-up area; and her blast always put out the dug-out candles. I relit 'em once, an' again at the end. In conclusion, this Macklin fell flat forward on 'is face, which was how 'e generally wound up 'is notion of a perfect day. Bosko absoluto!

"'Take 'im away," says 'Ammick to me. "'E's sufferin' from shell-shock."

'To cut a long story short, *that* was what first put the notion into my 'ead. Wouldn't it you? Even 'ad Macklin been a 'ighup Mason——'

'Wasn't 'e, then?' said Anthony, a little puzzled.

"'E'd never gone beyond the Blue Degrees, 'e told me. Any'ow, 'e'd lectured 'is superior officers up an' down; 'e'd as good as called 'em fools most o' the time, in 'is toff's voice. I 'eard 'im an' I saw 'im. An' all he got was—me told off to put 'im to bed! And all on account o' Jane! Would *you* have let a thing like that get past you? Nor me, either! Next mornin', when his stummick was settled, I was at him full-cry to find out 'ow it was worked. Toff or no toff, 'e knew his end of a bargain. First, 'e wasn't takin' any. He said I wasn't fit to be initiated into the Society of the Janeites. That only meant five bob more—fifteen up to date.

"'Make it one Bradbury,'" 'e says. "It's dirt-cheap. You saw me 'old the Circus in the 'ollow of me 'and?"

'No denyin' it. I *'ad*. So, for one pound, he communicated me the Password of the First Degree, which was *Tilniz an' trap-doors.*

"'I know what a trap-door is," I says to 'im, "but what in 'ell's *Tilniz?*"

"'You obey orders,'" 'e says, "an' next time I ask you what you're thinkin' about you'll answer, '*Tilniz an' trap-doors,*' in a smart and soldierly manner. I'll spring that question at me own time. All you've got to do is to be distinck."

'We settled all this while we was skinnin' spuds for dinner at the back o' the rear-truck under our camouflage-screens. Gawd, 'ow that glue-paint did stink! Otherwise, 'twasn't so bad, with the sun comin' through our pantomime-leaves, an' the wind marcelling the grasses in the cutting. Well, one thing leading to another, nothin' further 'appened in this direction till the afternoon. We 'ad a high standard o' livin' in Mess—an' in the Group, for that matter. I was talon' away Mosses lunch—dinner 'e would never call it—an' Mosse was fillin' 'is cigarette-case previous to the afternoon's duty. Macklin, in the passage, comin' in as if 'e didn't know Mosse was there, slings 'is question at me, an' I give the countersign in a low but quite distinck voice, makin' as if I 'adn't seen Mosse. Mosse looked at me through and through, with his cigarette-case in his 'and. Then 'e jerks out 'arf a dozen—best Turkish—on the table an' exits. I pinched 'em an' divvied with Macklin.

"'You see 'ow it works," says Macklin. "Could you 'ave invested a Bradbury to better advantage?"

"'So far, no," I says. "Otherwise, though, if they start provin' an' tryin' me, I'm a dead bird. There must be a lot more to this Janeite game."

"''Eaps an' 'eaps," he says. "But to show you the sort of 'eart I 'ave, I'll communicate you all the 'Igher Degrees among the Janeites, includin' the Charges, for another Bradbury; but you'll 'ave to work, Dobbin.'"

"Pretty free with your Bradburys, wasn't you?' Anthony grunted disapprovingly.

'What odds? *Ac*-tually, Gander told us, we couldn't expect to av'rage more than six weeks longer apiece, an', any'ow, *I* never regretted it. But make no mistake—the preparation was somethin' cruel. In the first place, I come under Macklin for direct instruction *re* Jane.'

'Oh! Jane *was* real, then?' Anthony glanced for an instant at me as he put the question. 'I couldn't quite make that out.'

'Real!' Humberstall's voice rose almost to a treble. 'Jane? Why, she was a little old maid 'oo'd written 'alf a dozen books about a hundred years ago. 'Twasn't as if there was anythin' *to* 'em, either. *I* know. I had to read 'em. They weren't adventurous, nor smutty, nor what you'd call even interestin'—all about girls o' seventeen (they begun young then, I tell you), not certain 'oom they'd like to marry; an' their dances an' card-parties an' picnics, and their young blokes goin' off to London on 'orseback for 'air-cuts an' shaves. It took a full day in those days, if you went to a proper barber. They wore wigs, too, when they was chemists or clergymen. All that interested me on account o' me profession, an' cuttin' the men's 'air every fortnight. Macklin used to chip me about bein' an 'air-dresser. 'E *could* pass remarks, too!'

Humberstall recited with relish a fragment of what must have been a superb commination-service, ending with, 'You lazy-minded, lousy-headed, long-trousered, perfumed perookier.'

'An' you took it?' Anthony's quick eyes ran over the man.

'Yes. I was after my money's worth; an' Macklin, havin' put 'is 'and to the plough, wasn't one to withdraw it. Otherwise, if I'd pushed 'im, I'd ha' slew 'im. Our Battery Sergeant Major nearly did. For Macklin had a wonderful way o' passing remarks on a man's civil life; an' he put it about that our B.S.M. had run a dope an' dolly-shop with a Chinese woman, the wrong end o' Southwark Bridge. Nothin' you could lay 'old of, o' course; but——' Humberstall let us draw our own conclusions.

'That reminds me,' said Anthony, smacking his lips. 'I 'ad a bit of a fracas with a fare in the Fulham Road last month. He called me a paras-tit-ic Forder. I informed 'im I was owner-driver, an' 'e could see for 'imself the cab was quite clean. That didn't suit 'im. 'E said it was crawlin'.'

'What happened?' I asked.

'One o' them blue-bellied Bolshies of postwar Police (neglectin' point-duty, as usual) asked us to flirt a little quieter. My joker chucked some Arabic at 'im. That was when we signed the Armistice. 'E'd been a Yeoman—a perishin' Gloucestershire Yeoman—that I'd helped gather in the orange crop with at Jaffa, in the 'Oly Land!'

'And after that?' I continued.

'It 'ud be 'ard to say. I know 'e lived at Hendon or Cricklewood. I drove 'im there. We must 'ave talked Zionism or somethin', because at seven next mornin' him an' me was tryin' to get petrol out of a milkshop at St. Albans. They 'adn't any. In lots o' ways this war has been a public noosance, as one might say, but there's no denyin' it 'elps you slip through life easier. The dairyman's son 'ad done time on Jordan with camels. So he stood us rum an' milk.'

'Just like 'avin' the Password, eh?' was Humberstall's comment.

'That's right! Ours was *Imshee kelb*. Not so 'ard to remember as your Jane stuff.'

'Jane wasn't so very 'ard—not the way Macklin used to put 'er,' Humberstall resumed. 'I 'ad only six books to remember. I learned the names by 'eart as Macklin placed 'em. There was one called *Persuasion*, first; an' the rest in a bunch, except another about some Abbey or other—last by three lengths. But, as I was sayin', what beat me was there was nothin' *to* 'em nor *in* 'em. Nothin' at all, believe me.'

'You seem good an' full of 'em, any'ow,' said Anthony.

'I mean that 'er characters was no *use*! They was only just like people you run across any day. One of 'em was a curate—the Reverend Collins—always on the make an' lookin' to marry money. Well, when I was a Boy Scout, 'im or 'is twin brother was our troop-leader. An' there was an upstandin' 'ard-mouthed Duchess or a Baronet's wife that didn't give a curse for any one 'oo wouldn't do what she told 'em to; the Lady—Lady Catherine (I'll get it in a minute) De Bugg. Before Ma bought the 'airdressin' business in London I used to know of an 'olesale grocer's wife near Leicester (I'm Leicestershire myself) that might 'ave been 'er duplicate. And—oh yes—there was a Miss Bates; just an old maid runnin' about like a hen with 'er 'ead cut off, an' her tongue loose at both ends. I've got an aunt like 'er. Good as gold—but, *you* know.'

'Lord, yes!' said Anthony, with feeling. 'An' did you find out what *Tilniz* meant? I'm always huntin' after the meanin' of things mesel'

'Yes, 'e was a swine of a Major-General, retired, and on the make. They're all on the make, in a quiet way, in Jane. 'E was so much of a gentleman by 'is own estimation that 'e was always be'avin' like a hound. *You* know the sort. 'Turned a girl out of 'is own 'ouse because she 'adn't any money—*after*, mark you, encouragin' 'er to set 'er cap at his son, because 'e thought she had.'

'But that 'appens all the time,' said Anthony. 'Why, me own mother——'

'That's right. So would mine. But this Tilney was a man, an' some'ow Jane put it down all so naked it made you ashamed. I told Macklin that, an' he said I was shapin' to be a good Janeite. 'Twasn't *his* fault if I wasn't. 'Nother thing, too; 'avin' been at the Bath Mineral Waters 'Ospital in 'Sixteen, with trench-feet, was a great advantage to me, because I knew the names o' the streets where Jane 'ad lived. There was one of 'em—Laura, I think, or some other girl's name—which Macklin said was 'oly ground. "If you'd been initiated *then*," he says, "you'd ha' felt your flat feet tingle every time you walked over those sacred pavin'-stones."

'"My feet tingled right enough," I said, "but not on account of Jane. Nothin' remarkable about that," I says.

'"Eaven lend me patience!" he says, combin' 'is 'air with 'is little hands. "Every dam' thing about Jane is remarkable to a pukka Janeite! It was there," he says, "that Miss What's—her Name" (he had the name; I've forgotten it) "made up 'er engagement again, after nine years, with Captain T'other Bloke." An' he dished me out a page an' a half of one of the books to learn by 'eart—*Persuasion*, I think it was.'

'You quick at gettin' things off by 'eart?' Anthony demanded.

'Not as a rule. I was then, though, or else Macklin knew 'ow to deliver the Charges properly. 'E said 'e'd been some sort o' schoolmaster

45

once, and he'd make my mind resume work or break 'imself. That was just before the Battery Sergeant-Major 'ad it in for him on account o' what he'd been sayin' about the Chinese wife an' the dollyshop.'

'What did Macklin really say?' Anthony and I asked together. Humberstall gave us a fragment. It was hardly the stuff to let loose on a pious post-war world without revision.

'And what had your B.S.M. been in civil life?' I asked at the end.

"'Ead-embalmer to an 'olesale undertaker in the Midlands,' said Humberstall; 'but, o' course, *when* he thought 'e saw his chance he naturally took it. He came along one mornin' lickin' 'is lips. "You don't get past me this time," 'e says to Macklin. "You're for it, Professor."

"'Ow so, me gallant Major," says Macklin; "an' what for?"

"'For writin' obese words on the breech o' the ten-inch," says the B.S.M. She was our old Skoda that I've been tellin' you about. We called 'er "Bloody Eliza." She 'ad a badly wore obturator an' blew through a fair treat. I knew by Macklin's face the B.S.M. 'ad dropped it somewhere, but all he vow'saifed was, "Very good, Major. We will consider it in Common Room," The B.S.M, couldn't ever stand Macklin's toff's way o' puttin' things; so he goes off rumblin' like 'ell's bells in an 'urricane, as the Marines say. Macklin put it to me at once, what had I been doin'? Some'ow he could read me like a book.

'Well, all I'd done—an' I told 'im *he* was responsible for it—was to chalk the guns. 'Ammick never minded what the men wrote up on 'em. 'E said it gave 'em an interest in their job. You'd see all sorts of remarks chalked on the sideplates or the gear-casin's.'

'What sort of remarks?' said Anthony keenly.

46

'Oh! 'Ow Bloody Eliza, or Spittin' Jim—that was our old Mark Five Nine-point-two—felt that morning, an' such things. But it 'ad come over me—more to please Macklin than anythin' else—that it was time we Janeites 'ad a look in. So, as I was tellin' you, I'd taken an' rechristened all three of 'em, on my own, early that mornin'. Spittin' Jim I 'ad chalked "The Reverend Collins"—that Curate I was tellin' you about; an' our cut-down Navy Twelve, "General Tilney," because it was worse wore in the groovin' than anything *I'd* ever seen. The Skoda (an' that was where *I* dropped it) I 'ad chalked up "The Lady Catherine De Bugg." I made a clean breast of it all to Macklin. He reached up an' patted me on the shoulder. "You done nobly," he says. "You're bringin' forth abundant fruit, like a good Janeite. But I'm afraid your spellin' has misled our worthy B.S.M. *That's* what it is," 'e says, slappin' 'is little leg. "'Ow might you 'ave spelt De Bourgh for example?"

'I told 'im. 'Twasn't right; an' 'e nips off to the Skoda to make it so. When 'e comes back, 'e says that the Gander 'ad been before 'im an' corrected the error. But we two come up before the Major, just the same, that afternoon after lunch ; 'Ammick in the chair, so to speak, Mosse in another, an' the B.S.M, chargin' Macklin with writin' obese words on His Majesty's property, on active service. When it transpired that me an' not Macklin was the offendin' party, the B.S.M, turned 'is hand in and sulked like a baby. 'E as good as told 'Ammick 'e couldn't hope to preserve discipline unless examples was made—meanin', o' course, Macklin.'

'Yes, I've heard all that,' said Anthony, with a contemptuous grunt. 'The worst of it is, a lot of it's true.'

"Ammick took 'im up sharp about Military Law, which he said was even more fair than the civilian article.'

'My Gawd!' This came from Anthony's scornful midmost bosom.

"'Accordin' to the unwritten law of the 'Eavies," says 'Ammick, "there's no objection to the men chalkin' the guns, if decency is preserved.

On the other 'and," says he, "we 'aven't yet settled the precise status of individuals entitled so to do. I 'old that the privilege is confined to combatants only."

"'With the permission of the Court," says Mosse, who was another born lawyer, "I'd like to be allowed to join issue on that point. Prisoner's position is very delicate an' doubtful, an' he has no legal representative."

"'Very good," says 'Ammick. "Macklin bein' acquitted——"

"'With submission, me lud," says Mosse. "I hope to prove 'e was accessory before the fact."

"'*As* you please," says 'Ammick. "But in that case, 'oo the 'ell's goin' to get the port I'm tryin' to stand the Court?"

"'I submit," says Mosse, "prisoner, bein' under direct observation o' the Court, could be temporarily enlarged for that duty."

'So Macklin went an' got it, an' the B.S.M. had 'is glass with the rest. Then they argued whether mess servants an' non-combatants was entitled to chalk the guns ('Ammick *versus* Mosse). After a bit, 'Ammick as C.O. give 'imself best, an' me an' Macklin was severely admonished for trespassin' on combatants' rights, an' the B.S.M. was warned that if we repeated the offence 'e could deal with us summ'rily. He 'ad some glasses o' port an' went out quite 'appy. Then my turn come, while Macklin was gettin' them their tea; an' one thing leadin' to another, 'Ammick put me through all the Janeite Degrees, you might say. 'Never 'ad such a doin' m my life.'

'Yes, but what did you tell 'em?' said Anthony. 'I can't ever *think* my lies quick enough when I'm for it.'

'No need to lie. I told 'em that the backside view o' the Skoda, when she was run up, put Lady De Bugg into my 'ead. They gave me right there, but they said I was wrong about General Tilney. 'Cordin' to them, our Navy twelve-inch ought to 'ave been christened Miss Bates. I said the same idea 'ad crossed my mind, till I'd seen the General's groovin'. Then I felt it had to be the General or nothin'. But they give me full marks for the Reverend Collins—our Nine-point-two.'

'An' you fed 'em *that* sort o' talk?' Anthony's fox-coloured eyebrows climbed almost into his hair.

'While I was assistin' Macklin to get tea—yes. Seem' it was an examination, I wanted to do 'im credit as a Janeite.'

'An'—an' what did they say?'

'They said it was 'ighly creditable to us both. I don't drink, so they give me about a hundred fags.'

'Gawd! What a Circus you must 'ave been,' was Anthony's gasping comment.

'It *was* a 'appy little Group. I wouldn't 'a changed with any other.'

Humberstall sighed heavily as he helped Anthony slide back the organ-panel. We all admired it in silence, while Anthony repocketed his secret polishing mixture, which lived in a tin tobacco-box. I had neglected my work for listening to Humberstall. Anthony reached out quietly and took over a Secretary's jewel and a rag. Humberstall studied his reflection in the glossy wood.

'Almost,' he said critically, holding his head to one side.

'Not with an Army. You could with a Safety, though,' said Anthony. And, indeed, as Brother Burges had foretold, one might have shaved in it with comfort.

'Did you ever run across any of 'em afterwards, any time?' Anthony asked presently.

'Not so many of 'em left to run after, now. With the 'Eavies it's mostly neck or nothin'. We copped it. In the neck. In due time.'

'Well, *you* come out of it all right.' Anthony spoke both stoutly and soothingly; but Humberstall would not be comforted.

'That's right; but I almost wish I 'adn't,' he sighed. 'I was 'appier there than ever before or since. Jerry's March push in 'Eighteen did us in; an' yet, 'ow could we 'ave expected it? 'Ow *could* we 'ave expected it? We'd been sent back for rest an' runnin'-repairs, back pretty near our base; an' our old loco' that used to shift us about o' nights, she'd gone down the line for repairs. But for 'Ammick we wouldn't even 'ave 'ad our camouflage-screens up. He told our Brigadier that, whatever 'e might be in the Gunnery line, as a leadin' Divorce lawyer he never threw away a point in argument. So 'e 'ad us all screened in over in a cuttin' on a little spur-line near a wood; an' 'e saw to the screens 'imself. The leaves weren't more than comin' out then, an' the sun used to make our glue-paint stink. Just like actin' in a theatre, it was! But 'appy. *But* 'appy! I expect if we'd been caterpillars, like the new big six-inch hows, they'd ha' remembered us. But we was the old La Bassée '15 Mark o' Heavies that ran on rails— not much more good than scrap-iron that late in the war. An', believe me, gents—or Brethren, as I should say—we copped it cruel. Look 'ere! It was in the afternoon, an' I was watchin' Gander instructin' a class in new sights at Lady Catherine. All of a sudden I 'eard our screens rip overhead, an' a runner on a motor-bike come sailin', sailin' through the air—like that bloke that used to bicycle off Brighton Pier—and landed one awful wop almost atop o' the class. '"Old 'ard," says Gander. "That's no way to report. What's the fuss?" "Your screens 'ave broke my back, for one

50

thing," says the bloke on the ground; "an' for another, the 'ole front's gone." "Nonsense," says Gander. 'E 'adn't more than passed the remark when the man was vi'lently sick an' conked out. 'E 'ad plenty papers on 'im from Brigadiers and C.O.'s reporting 'emselves cut off an' askin' for orders. 'E was right both ways—his back an' our front. The 'ole Somme front washed out as clean as kiss-me-'and!' His huge hand smashed down open on his knee.

'We 'eard about it at the time in the 'Oly Land. Was it reelly as quick as all that?' said Anthony.

'Quicker! Look 'ere! The motor—bike dropped in on us about four pip-emma. After that, we tried to get orders o' some kind or other, but nothin' came through excep' that all available transport was in use and not likely to be released. *That* didn't 'elp us any. About nine o'clock comes along a young Brass 'At in brown gloves. We was quite a surprise to 'im. 'E said they were evacuating the area and we'd better shift. "Where to?" says 'Ammick, rather short.

"'Oh, somewhere Amiens way," he says. "Not that I'd guarantee Amiens for any length o' time; but Amiens might do to begin with." I'm giving you the very words. Then 'e goes off swingin' 'is brown gloves, and 'Ammick sends for Gander and orders 'im to march the men through Amiens to Dieppe; book thence to New'aven, take up positions be'ind Seaford, an' carry on the war. Gander said 'e'd see 'im damned first. 'Ammick says 'e'd see 'im courtmartialled after. Gander says what 'e meant to say was that the men 'ud see all an' sundry damned before they went into Amiens with their gunsights wrapped up in their puttees. 'Ammick says 'e 'adn't said a word about puttees, an' carryin' off the gunsights was purely optional. "Well, anyhow," says Gander, "puttees *or* drawers, they ain't goin' to shift a step unless you lead the procession."

"'Mutinous 'ounds," says 'Amrnick. "But we live in a democratic age. D'you suppose they'd object to kindly diggin' 'emselves in a bit?" "Not at all," says Gander. "The B.S.M.'s kept 'em at it like terriers for the last three hours." "That bein' so," says 'Ammick, "Macklin'll now fetch us small glasses o' port." Then Mosse comes in—he could smell port a mile off—an' he submits we'd only add to the congestion in Amiens if we took our crowd there, whereas, if we lay doggo where we was, Jerry might miss us, though he didn't seem to be missin' much that evenin'.

'The 'ole country was pretty noisy, an' our dumps we'd lit ourselves flarin' heavens-high as far as you could see. Lyin' doggo was our best chance. I believe we might ha' pulled it off, if we'd been left alone, but along towards midnight—there was some small stuff swishin' about, but nothin' particular—a nice little bald-headed old gentleman in uniform pushes into the dug-out wipin' his glasses an' sayin' 'e was thinkin' o' formin' a defensive flank on our left with 'is battalion which 'ad just come up. 'Ammick says 'e wouldn't form much if 'e was 'im. "Oh, don't say *that*," says the old gentleman, very shocked. "One must support the Guns, mustn't one?" "'Ammick says we was refittin' an' about as effective, just then, as a public lav'tory. "Go into Amiens," he says, "an' defend 'em there." "Oh no," says the old gentleman, "me an' my laddies *must* make a defensive flank for you," an' he flips out of the dug-out like a performin' bullfinch, chirruppin' for his "laddies." Gawd in 'Eaven knows what sort o' push they was—little boys mostly—but they 'ung on to 'is coat-tails like a Sunday-school treat, an' we 'eard 'em muckin' about in the open for a bit. Then a pretty tight barrage was slapped down for ten minutes, an' 'Ammick thought the laddies had copped it already. "It'll be our turn next," says Mosse. "There's been a covey o' Gothas messin' about for the last 'alf-hour—lookin' for the Railway Shops, I expect. They're just as likely to take us." "Arisin' out o' that," says 'Ammick, "one of 'em sounds pretty low down now. We're for it, me learned colleagues!" "Jesus!" says Gander, "I believe you're right, sir." And that was the last word *I* 'eard on the matter.'

'Did they cop you then?' said Anthony.

'They did. I expect Mosse was right, an' they took us for the Railway Shops. When I come to, I was lyin' outside the cuttin', which was pretty well filled up. The Reverend Collins was all right; but Lady Catherine and the General was past prayin' for. I lay there, takin' it in, till I felt cold an' I looked at meself. Otherwise, I 'adn't much on excep' me boots. So I got up an' walked about to keep warm. Then I saw somethin' like a mushroom in the moonlight. It was the nice old gentleman's bald 'ead. I patted it. 'im and 'is laddies 'ad copped it right enough. Some battalion run out in a 'urry from England, I suppose. They 'adn't even begun to dig in—pore little perishers! I dressed myself off 'em there, an' topped off with a British warm. Then I went back to the cuttin' an' someone says to me: "Dig, you ox, dig! Gander's under." So I 'elped shift things till I threw up blood an' bile mixed. Then I dropped, an' they brought Gander out—dead—an' laid 'im next me. 'Ammick 'ad gone too—fair tore in 'alf, the B.S.M. said; but the funny thing was he talked quite a lot before 'e died, an' nothin' to 'im below 'is stummick, they told me. Mosse we never found. 'E'd been standing by Lady Catherine. She'd up-ended an' gone back on 'em, with 'alf the cuttin' atop of 'er, by the look of things.'

'And what come to Macklin?' said Anthony.

'Dunno. . . . 'E was with 'Ammick. I expect I must ha' been blown clear of all by the first bomb; for I was the on'y Janeite left. We lost about half our crowd, either under, or after we'd got 'em out. The B.S.M. went off 'is rocker when mornin' came, an' he ran about from one to another sayin' : "That was a good push! That was a great crowd! Did ye ever know any push to touch 'em?" An' then 'e'd cry. So what was left of us made off for ourselves, an' I came across a lorry, pretty full, but they took me in.'

'Ah!' said Anthony with pride. '"They all take a taxi when it's rainin'." 'Ever 'eard that song?'

'They went a long way back. Then I walked a bit, an' there was a hospital-train fillin' up, an' one of the Sisters—a grey-headed one—ran at me wavin' 'er red 'ands an' sayin' there wasn't room for a louse in it. I was past carin'. But she went on talkin' and talkin' about the war, an' her pa in Ladbroke Grove, an' 'ow strange for 'er at 'er time of life to be doin' this work with a lot o' men, an' next war, 'ow the nurses 'ud 'ave to wear khaki breeches on account o' the mud, like the Land Girls; an' that reminded 'er, she'd boil me an egg if she could lay 'ands on one, for she'd run a chicken-farm once. You never 'eard anythin' like it—outside o' Jane. It set me off laughin' again. Then a woman with a nose an' teeth on 'er, marched up. "What's all this?" she says. "What do you want?" "Nothing," I says, "only make Miss Bates, there, stop talkin' or I'll die." "Miss Bates?" she says. "What in 'Eaven's name makes you call 'er that?" "Because she is," I says. "D'you know what you're sayin'?" she says, an' slings her bony arm round me to get me off the ground. "'Course I do," I says, "an' if you knew Jane you'd know too." "That's enough," says she. "You're comin' on this train if I have to kill a Brigadier for you," an' she an' an ord'ly fair hove me into the train, on to a stretcher close to the cookers. That beef-tea went down well! Then she shook 'ands with me an' said I'd hit off Sister Molyneux in one, an' then she pinched me an extra blanket. It was 'er own 'ospital pretty much. I expect she was the Lady Catherine de Bourgh of the area. Well, an' so, to cut a long story short, nothing further transpired.'

"Adn't you 'ad enough by then?' asked Anthony.

'I expect so. Otherwise, if the old Circus 'ad been carryin' on, I might 'ave 'ad another turn with 'em before Armistice. Our B.S.M. was right. There never was a 'appier push. 'Ammick an' Mosse an' Gander an' the B.S.M. an' that pore little Macklin man makin' an' passin' an' raisin' me an' gettin' me on to the 'ospital train after 'e was dead, all for a couple of Bradburys. I lie awake nights still, reviewing matters. There never was a push to touch ours—never!'

Anthony handed me back the Secretary's Jewel resplendent.

'Ah,' said he. 'No denyin' that Jane business was more useful to you than the Roman Eagles or the Star an' Garter. 'Pity there wasn't any of you Janeites in the 'Oly Land. I never come across 'em.'

'Well, as pore Macklin said, it's a very select Society, an' you've got to be a Janeite in your 'eart, or you won't have any success. An' yet he made *me* a Janeite! I read all her six books now for pleasure 'tween times in the shop; an' it brings it all back—down to the smell of the glue-paint on the screens. You take it from me, Brethren, there's no one to touch Jane when you're in a tight place. Gawd bless 'er, whoever she was.'

Worshipful Brother Burges, from the floor of the Lodge, called us all from Labour to Refreshment. Humberstall hove himself up—so very a cart-horse of a man one almost expected to hear the harness creak on his back—and descended the steps.

He said he could not stay for tea because he had promised his mother to come home for it, and she would most probably be waiting for him now at the Lodge door.

'One or other of 'em always comes for 'im. He's apt to miss 'is gears sometimes,' Anthony explained to me, as we followed.

'Goes on a bust, d'you mean?'

'Im! He's no more touched liquor than 'e 'as women since 'e was born. No, 'e's liable to a sort o' quiet fits, like. They came on after the dump blew up at Eatables. But for them, 'e'd ha' been Battery Sergeant-Major.'

'Oh!' I said. 'I couldn't make out why he took on as mess-waiter when he got back to his guns. That explains things a bit.'

''Is sister told me the dump goin' up knocked all 'is Gunnery instruction clean out of 'im. The only thing 'e stuck to was to get back to

55

'is old crowd. Gawd knows 'ow 'e worked it, but 'e did. He fair deserted out of England to 'em, she says; an' when they saw the state 'e was in, they 'adn't the 'eart to send 'im back or into 'ospital. They kep' 'im for a mascot, as you might say. That's *all* dead-true. 'Is sister told me so. But I can't guarantee that Janeite business, excep' 'e never told a lie since 'e was six. 'Is sister told me so. What do *you* think?'

'He isn't likely to have made it up out of his own head,' I replied.

'But people don't get so crazy-fond o' books as all that, do they? 'E's made 'is sister try to read 'em. She'd do anythin' to please him. But, as I keep tellin' 'er, so'd 'is mother. D'you 'appen to know anything about Jane?'

'I believe Jane was a bit of a match-maker in a quiet way when she was alive, and I know all her books are full of match-making,' I said. '*You'd* better look out.'

'Oh, *that's* as good as settled,' Anthony replied, blushing.

A MADONNA OF THE TRENCHES

'Whatever a man of the sons of men
Shall say to his heart of the lords above,
They have shown man, verily, once and again,
Marvelous mercies and infinite love.

.   .   .   .   .

'O sweet one love, O my life's delight,
Dear, though the days have divided us,
Lost beyond hope, taken far out of sight,
Not twice in the world shall the Gods do thus.'
SWINBURNE, *'Les Novades'*

Seeing how many unstable ex-soldiers came to the Lodge of Instruction (attached to Faith and Works E.C. 5837*) in the years after the war, the wonder is there was not more trouble from Brethren whom sudden meetings with old comrades jerked back into their still raw past. But our round, torpedo-bearded local Doctor—Brother Keede, Senior Warden—always stood ready to deal with hysteria before it got out of hand; and when I examined Brethren unknown or imperfectly vouched for on the Masonic side, I passed on to him anything that seemed doubtful. He had had his experience as medical officer of a South London Battalion, during the last two years of the war; and, naturally, often found friends and acquaintances among the visitors.

Brother C. Strangwick, a young, tallish, new-made Brother, hailed from some South London Lodge. His papers and his answers were above suspicion, but his red-rimmed eyes had a puzzled glare that might mean nerves. So I introduced him particularly to Keede, who discovered in him a Headquarters Orderly of his old Battalion, congratulated him on his return to fitness—he had been discharged for some infirmity or other—and plunged at once into Somme memories.

'I hope I did right, Keede,' I said when we were robing before Lodge.

'Oh, quite. He reminded me that I had him under my hands at Sampoux in 'Eighteen, when he went to bits. He was a Runner.'

'Was it shock?' I asked.

'Of sorts—but not what he wanted me to think it was. No, he wasn't shamming. He had jumps to the limit—but he played up to mislead me about the reason of 'em . . . . Well, if we could stop patients from lying, medicine would be too easy, I suppose.'

I noticed that, after Lodge-working, Keede gave him a seat a couple of rows in front of us, that he might enjoy a lecture on the Orientation of King Solomon's Temple, which an earnest Brother thought would be a nice interlude between Labour and the high tea that we called our 'Banquet.' Even helped by tobacco it was a dreary performance. About half-way through, Strangwick, who had been fidgeting and twitching for some minutes, rose, drove back his chair grinding across the tesselated floor, and yelped 'Oh, My Aunt! I can't stand this any longer.' Under cover of a general laugh of assent he brushed past us and stumbled towards the door.

'I thought so!' Keede whispered to me. 'Come along!' We overtook him in the passage, crowing hysterically and wringing his hands. Keede led him into the Tyler's Room, a small office where we stored odds and ends of regalia and furniture, and locked the door.

'I'm—I'm all right,' the boy began, piteously.

"Course you are.' Keede opened a small cupboard which I had seen called upon before, mixed sal volatile and water in a graduated glass, and, as Strangwick drank, pushed him gently on to an old sofa. 'There,' he went on. 'It's nothing to write home about. I've seen you ten times worse. I expect our talk has brought things back.'

He hooked up a chair behind him with one foot, held the patient's hands in his own, and sat down. The chair creaked.

'Don't!' Strangwick squealed. 'I can't stand it! There's nothing on earth creaks like they do! And—and when it thaws we—we've got to slap 'em back with a spa-ade ! 'Remember those Frenchmen's little boots under the duckboards? . . . What'll I do? What'll I do about it?'

Some one knocked at the door, to know if all were well.

'Oh, quite, thanks!' said Keede over his shoulder. 'But I shall need this room awhile. Draw the curtains, please.'

We heard the rings of the hangings that drape the passage from Lodge to Banquet Room click along their poles, and what sound there had been, of feet and voices, was shut off.

Strangwick, retching impotently, complained of the frozen dead who creak in the frost.

'He's playing up still,' Keede whispered. '*That's* not his real trouble—any more than 'twas last time.'

'But surely,' I replied, 'men get those things on the brain pretty badly. 'Remember in October——'

'This chap hasn't, though. I wonder what's really helling him. What are you thinking of?' said Keede peremptorily.

'French End an' Butcher's Row,' Strangwick muttered.

'Yes, there were a few there. But suppose we face Bogey instead of giving him best every time.' Keede turned towards me with a hint in his eye that I was to play up to his leads.

'What was the trouble with French End?' I opened at a venture.

'It was a bit by Sampoux, that we had taken over from the French. They're tough, but you wouldn't call 'em tidy as a nation. They had faced both sides of it with dead to keep the mud back. All those trenches were like gruel in a thaw. Our people had to do the same sort of thing— elsewhere; but Butcher's Row in French End was the—er—show-piece. Luckily, we pinched a salient from Jerry just then, an' straightened things out—so we didn't need to use the Row after November. You remember, Strangwick?'

'My God, yes! When the Buckboard-slats were missin' you'd tread on 'em, an' they'd creak.'

'They're bound to. Like leather,' said Keede. 'It gets on one's nerves a bit, but——'

'Nerves? It's real! It's real!' Strangwick gulped.

'But at your time of life, it'll all fall behind you in a year or so. I'll give you another sip of—paregoric, an' we'll face it quietly. Shall we?'

Keede opened his cupboard again and administered a carefully dropped dark dose of something that was not sal volatile. 'This'll settle you in a few minutes,' he explained. 'Lie still, an' don't talk unless you feel like it.'

He faced me, fingering his beard.

'Ye-es. Butcher's Row wasn't pretty,' he volunteered. 'Seeing Strangwick here, has brought it all back to me again. 'Funny thing! We had a Platoon Sergeant of Number Two—what the deuce was his name?—an elderly bird who must have lied like a patriot to get out to the front at his age; but he was a first-class Non-Com., and the last person, you'd think, to make mistakes. Well, he was due for a fortnight's home

60

leave in January, 'Eighteen. You were at B.H.Q. then, Strangwick, weren't you?'

'Yes. I was Orderly. It was January twenty-first'; Strangwick spoke with a thickish tongue, and his eyes burned. Whatever drug it was, had taken hold.

'About then,' Keede said. 'Well, this Sergeant, instead of coming down from the trenches the regular way an' joinin' Battalion Details after dark, an' takin' that funny little train for Arras, thinks he'll warm himself first. So he gets into a dug-out, in Butcher's Row, that used to be an old French dressing-station, and fugs up between a couple of braziers of pure charcoal! As luck 'ud have it, that was the only dug-out with an inside door opening inwards—some French anti-gas fitting, I expect—and, by what we could make out, the door must have swung to while he was warming. Anyhow, he didn't turn up at the train. There was a search at once. We couldn't afford to waste Platoon Sergeants. We found him in the morning. He'd got his gas all right. A machine-gunner reported him, didn't he, Strangwick?'

'No, Sir. Corporal Grant—o' the Trench Mortars.'

'So it was. Yes, Grant—the man with that little wen on his neck. 'Nothing wrong with your memory, at any rate. What was the Sergeant's name?'

'Godsoe—John Godsoe,' Strangwick answered.

'Yes, that was it. I had to see him next mornin'—frozen stiff between the two braziers—and not a scrap of private papers on him. *That* was the only thing that made me think it mightn't have been— quite an accident.'

Strangwick's relaxing face set, and he threw back at once to the Orderly Room manner.

'I give my evidence—at the time—to you, sir. He passed—overtook me, I should say—comin' down from supports, after I'd warned him for leaf. I thought he was goin' through Parrot Trench as usual; but 'e must 'ave turned off into French End where the old bombed barricade was.'

'Yes. I remember now. You were the last man to see him alive. That was on the twenty-first of January, you say? Now, *when* was it that Dearlove and Billings brought you to me—clean out of your head?' ... Keede dropped his hand, in the style of magazine detectives, on Strangwick's shoulder. The boy looked at him with cloudy wonder, and muttered: 'I was took to you on the evenin' of the twenty-fourth of January. But you don't think I did him in, do you?'

I could not help smiling at Keede's discomfiture; but he recovered himself. 'Then what the dickens *was* on your mind that evening—before I gave you the hypodermic?'

'The—the things in Butcher's Row. They kept on comin' over me. You've seen me like this before, sir.'

'But I knew that it was a lie. You'd no more got stiffs on the brain then than you have now. You've got something, but you're hiding it.'

"Ow do *you* know, Doctor?' Strangwick whimpered.

'D'you remember what you said to me, when Dearlove and Billings were holding you down that evening?'

'About the things in Butcher's Row?'

'Oh, no! You spun me a lot of stuff about corpses creaking; but you let yourself go in the middle of it—when you pushed that telegram at me. What did you mean, f'rinstance, by asking what advantage it was for you to fight beasts of officers if the dead didn't rise?'

'Did I say "Beasts of Officers"?'

'You did. It's out of the Burial Service.'

'I suppose, then, I must have heard it. As a matter of fact, I 'ave.'
Strangwick shuddered extravagantly.

'Probably. And there's another thing—that hymn you were
shouting till I put you under. It was something about Mercy and Love.
'Remember it?'

'I'll try,' said the boy obediently, and began to paraphrase, as
nearly as possible thus: '"Whatever a man may say in his heart unto the
Lord, yea, verily I say unto you—Gawd hath shown man, again and again,
marvellous mercy an'—an' somethin' or other love."' He screwed up his
eyes and shook.

'Now where did you get *that* from?' Keede insisted.

'From Godsoe—on the twenty-first Jan . . . . 'Ow could I tell what
'e meant to do?' he burst out in a high, unnatural key—'Any more than I
knew *she* was dead.'

'Who was dead?' said Keede.

'Me Auntie Armine.'

'The one the telegram came to you about, at Sampoux, that you
wanted me to explain—the one that you were talking of in the passage
out here just now when you began: "O Auntie," and changed it to "O
Gawd," when I collared you?'

'That's her! I haven't a chance with you, Doctor. *I* didn't know
there was anything wrong with those braziers. How could I? We're always
usin' 'em. Honest to God, I thought at first go-off he might wish to warm

himself before the leaf-train. I—I didn't know Uncle John meant to start—'ouse-keepin'.' He laughed horribly, and then the dry tears came.

Keede waited for them to pass in sobs and hiccoughs before he continued: 'Why? Was Godsoe your Uncle?'

'No,' said Strangwick, his head between his hands. 'Only we'd known him ever since we were born. Dad 'ad known him before that. He lived almost next street to us. Him an' Dad an' Ma an'—an' the rest had always been friends. So we called him Uncle—like children do.'

'What sort of man was he?'

'One o' *the* best, sir. 'Pensioned Sergeant with a little money left him—quite independent—and very superior. They had a sittin'-room full o' Indian curios that him and his wife used to let sister an' me see when we'd been good.'

'Wasn't he rather old to join up?'

'That made no odds to him. He joined up as Sergeant Instructor at the first go-off, an' when the Battalion was ready he got 'imself sent along. He wangled me into 'is Platoon when I went out—early in 'Seventeen. Because Ma wanted it, I suppose.'

'I'd no notion you knew him that well,' was Keede's comment.

'Oh, it made no odds to him. He 'ad no pets in the Platoon, but 'e'd write 'ome to Ma about me an' all the doin's. You see'—Strangwick stirred uneasily on the sofa—'we'd known him all our lives—lived in the next street an' all . . . . An' him well over fifty. Oh dear me! *Oh* dear me! What a bloody mix-up things are, when one's as young as me!' he wailed of a sudden.

But Keede held him to the point. 'He wrote to your Mother about you?'

'Yes. Ma's eyes had gone bad followin' on air-raids. 'Blood-vessels broke behind 'em from sittin' in cellars an' bein' sick. She had to 'ave 'er letters read to her by Auntie. Now I think of it, that was the only thing that you might have called anything at all———'

'Was that the Aunt that died, and that you got the wire about?' Keede drove on.

'Yes—Auntie Armine—Ma's younger sister, an' she nearer fifty than forty. What a mix-up! An' if I'd been asked any time about it, I'd 'ave sworn there wasn't a single sol'tary item concernin' her that everybody didn't know an' hadn't known all along. No more conceal to her doin's than—than so much shop-front. She'd looked after sister an' me, when needful—whoopin' cough an' measles just the same as Ma. We was in an' out of her house like rabbits. You see, Uncle Armine is a cabinet-maker, an' second-'and furniture, an' we liked playin' with the things. She 'ad no children, and when the war came, she said she was glad of it. But she never talked much of her feelin's. She kept herself to herself, you understand.' He stared most earnestly at us to help out our understandings.

'What was she like?' Keede inquired.

'A biggish woman, an' had been 'andsome, I believe, but, bein' used to her, we two didn't notice much—except, per'aps, for one thing. Ma called her 'er proper name, which was Bella; but Sis an' me always called 'er Auntie Armine. See?'

'What for?'

'We thought it sounded more like her—like somethin' movin' slow, in armour.'

'Oh! And she read your letters to your mother, did she?'

'Every time the post came in she'd slip across the road from opposite an' read 'em. An'—an' I'll go bail for it that that was all there was to it for as far back as I remember. Was I to swing to-morrow, I'd go bail for *that*! 'Tisn't fair of 'em to 'ave unloaded it all on me, because—because—if the dead *do* rise, why, what in 'ell becomes of me an' all I've believed all me life? I want to know *that*! I—I——'

But Keede would not be put off. 'Did the Sergeant give you away at all in his letters?' he demanded, very quietly.

'There was nothin' to give away—we was too busy—but his letters about me were a great comfort to Ma. I'm no good at writin'. I saved it all up for my leafs. I got me fourteen days every six months an' one over . . . . I was luckier than most, that way.'

'And when you came home, used you to bring 'em news about the Sergeant?' said Keede.

'I expect I must have; but I didn't think much of it at the time. I was took up with me own affairs—naturally. Uncle John always wrote to me once each leaf, tellin' me what was doin' an' what I was li'ble to expect on return, an' Ma 'ud 'ave that read to her. Then o' course I had to slip over to his wife an' pass her the news. An' then there was the young lady that I'd thought of marryin' if I came through. We'd got as far as pricin' things in the windows together.'

'And you didn't marry her—after all?'

Another tremor shook the boy. '*No!*' he cried. "'Fore it ended, I knew what reel things reelly mean! I—I never dreamed such things could be! . . . An' she nearer fifty than forty an' me own Aunt! . . . But there wasn't a sign nor a hint from first to last, so 'ow *could* I tell? Don't you *see* it? All she said to me after me Christmas leaf in' '18, when I come to say good-bye—all Auntie Armine said to me was: "You'll be seein' Mister Godsoe soon?" "Too soon for my likings," I says. "Well then, tell 'im from me," she says, "that I expect to be through with my little trouble by the twenty-first of next month, an' I'm dyin' to see him as soon as possible after that date."'

'What sort of trouble was it?' Keede turned professional at once.

'She'd 'ad a bit of a gatherin' in 'er breast, I believe. But she never talked of 'er body much to any one.'

"see,' said Keede. 'And she said to you?'

Strangwick repeated: "'Tell Uncle John I hope to be finished of my drawback by the twenty-first, an' I'm dying to see 'im as soon as 'e can after that date." An' then she says, laughin': "But you've a head like a sieve. I'll write it down, an' you can give it him when you see 'im." So she wrote it on a bit o' paper an' I kissed 'er good-bye—I was always her favourite, you see—an' I went back to Sampoux. The thing hardly stayed in my mind at all, d'you see. But the next time I was up in the front line—I was a Runner, d'ye see—our platoon was in North Bay Trench an' I was up with a message to the Trench Mortar there that Corporal Grant was in charge of. Followin' on receipt of it, he borrowed a couple of men off the platoon, to slue 'er round or somethin'. I give Uncle John Auntie Armine's paper, an' I give Grant a fag, an' we warmed up a bit over a brazier. Then Grant says to me: "I don't like it"; an' he jerks 'is thumb at Uncle John in the bay studyin' Auntie's message. Well, *you* know, sir, you had to speak to Grant about 'is way of prophesyin' things—after Rankine shot himself with the Very light.'

'I did,' said Keede, and he explained to me 'Grant had the Second Sight—confound him! It upset the men. I was glad when he got pipped. What happened after that, Strangwick?'

'Grant whispers to me: "Look, you damned Englishman. 'E's for it." Uncle John was leanin' up against the bay, an' hummin' that hymn I was tryin' to tell you just now. He looked different all of a sudden—as if 'e'd got shaved. *I* don't know anything of these things, but I cautioned Grant as to his style of speakin', if an officer 'ad 'eard him, an' I went on. Passin' Uncle John in the bay, 'e nods an' smiles, which he didn't often, an' he says, pocketin' the paper "This suits *me*. I'm for leaf on the twenty-first, too."'

'He said that to you, did he?' said Keede.

'*Pre*cisely the same as passin' the time o' day. O' course I returned the agreeable about hopin' he'd get it, an' in due course I returned to 'Eadquarters. The thing 'ardly stayed in my mind a minute. That was the eleventh January—three days after I'd come back from leaf. You remember, sir, there wasn't anythin' doin' either side round Sampoux the first part o' the month. Jerry was gettin' ready for his March Push, an' as long as he kept quiet, we didn't want to poke 'im up.'

'I remember that,' said Keede. 'But what about the Sergeant?'

'I must have met him, on an' off, I expect, goin' up an' down, through the ensuin' days, but it didn't stay in me mind. Why needed it? And on the twenty-first Jan., his name was on the leaf-paper when I went up to warn the leaf-men. I noticed *that*, o' course. Now that very afternoon Jerry 'ad been tryin' a new trench-mortar, an' before our 'Eavies could out it, he'd got a stinker into a bay an' mopped up 'alf a dozen. They were bringin' 'em down when I went up to the supports, an' that blocked Little Parrot, same as it always did. *You* remember, sir?'

'Rather! And there was that big machine-gun behind the Half-House waiting for you if you got out,' said Keede.

'I remembered that too. But it was just on dark an' the fog was comin' off the Canal, so I hopped out of Little Parrot an' cut across the open to where those four dead Warwicks are heaped up. But the fog turned me round, an' the next thing I knew I was knee-over in that old 'alf-trench that runs west o' Little Parrot into French End. I dropped into it—almost atop o' the machine-gun platform by the side o' the old sugar boiler an' the two Zoo-ave skel'tons. That gave me my bearin's, an' so I went through French End, all up those missin' Buckboards, into Butcher's Row where the *poy-looz* was laid in six deep each side, an' stuffed under the Buckboards. It had froze tight, an' the drippin's had stopped, an' the creakin's had begun.'

'Did that really worry you at the time?' Keede asked.

'No,' said the boy with professional scorn. 'If a Runner starts noticin' such things he'd better chuck. In the middle of the Row, just before the old dressin'-station you referred to, sir, it come over me that somethin' ahead on the Buckboards was just like Auntie Armine, waitin' beside the door; an' I thought to meself 'ow truly comic it would be if she could be dumped where I was then. In 'alf a second I saw it was only the dark an' some rags o' gas-screen, 'angin' on a bit of board, 'ad played me the trick. So I went on up to the supports an' warned the leaf-men there, includin' Uncle John. Then I went up Rake Alley to warn 'em in the front line. I didn't hurry because I didn't want to get there till Jerry 'ad quieted down a bit. Well, then a Company Relief dropped in—an' the officer got the wind up over some lights on the flank, an' tied 'em into knots, an' I 'ad to hunt up me leaf-men all over the blinkin' shop. What with one thing an' another, it must 'ave been 'alf-past eight before I got back to the supports. There I run across Uncle John, scrapm' mud off himself, havin' shaved—quite the dandy. He asked about the Arras train, an' I said, if Jerry was quiet, it might be ten o'clock. "Good!" says 'e. "I'll come with you." So we started back down the old trench that used to run across Halnaker, back of the support dug-outs. *You* know, sir.'

Keede nodded.

'Then Uncle John says something to me about seein' Ma an' the rest of 'em in a few days, an' had I any messages for 'em? Gawd knows what made me do it, but I told 'im to tell Auntie Armine I never expected to see anything like *her* up in our part of the world. And while I told him I laughed. That's the last time I *'ave* laughed." Oh—you've seen 'er, 'ave you? says he, quite natural-like. Then I told 'im about the sand-bags an' rags in the dark, playin' the trick. "Very likely," says he, brushin' the mud off his putties. By this time, we'd got to the corner where the old barricade into French End was—before they bombed it down, sir. He turns right an' climbs across it. "No, thanks," says I. "I've been there once this evenin'." But he wasn't attendin' to me. He felt behind the rubbish an' bones just inside the barricade, an' when he straightened up, he had a full brazier in each hand.

'"Come on, Clem," he says, an' he very rarely give me me own name. "You aren't afraid, are you?" he says. "It's just as short, an' if Jerry starts up again he won't waste stuff here. He knows it's abandoned." "Who's afraid now?" I says. "Me for one," says he. "I don't want *my* leaf spoiled at the last minute." Then 'e wheels round an' speaks that bit you said come out o' the Burial Service.'

For some reason Keede repeated it in full, slowly: 'If after the manner of men I have fought with beasts at Ephesus, what advantageth it me, if the dead rise not?'

'That's it,' said Strangwick. 'So we went down French End together—everything froze up an' quiet, except for their creakin's. I remember thinkin'——' his eyes began to flicker.

'Don't think. Tell what happened,' Keede ordered.

'Oh! Beg y' pardon! He went on with his braziers, hummin' his hymn, down Butcher's Row. Just before we got to the old dressin' station he stops and sets 'em down an' says "Where did you say she was, Clem? Me eyes ain't as good as they used to be."

"'In 'er bed at 'ome," I says. "Come on down. It's perishin' cold, an' *I'm* not due for leaf."

"'Well, I am," 'e says. "*I* am. . . ." An' then—'give you me word I didn't recognise the voice—he stretches out 'is neck a bit, in a way 'e 'ad, an' he says: "Why, Bella!" 'e says. "Oh, Bella!" 'e says. "Thank Gawd!" 'e says. Just like that! An' then I saw—I tell you I saw—Auntie Armine herself standin' by the old dressin' station door where first I'd thought I'd seen her. He was lookin' at 'er an' she was lookin' at him. I saw it, an' me soul turned over inside me because—because it knocked out everything I'd believed in. I 'ad nothin' to lay 'old of, d'ye see? An' 'e was lookin' at 'er as though he could 'ave et 'er, an' she was lookin' at 'im the same way, out of 'er eyes. Then he says: "Why, Bella," 'e says, "this must be only the second time we've been alone together in all these years." An' I saw 'er half hold out her arms to 'im in that perishin' cold. An' she nearer fifty than forty an' me own Aunt! You can shop me for a lunatic to-morrow, but I saw it—I *saw* 'er answerin' to his spoken word . . . Then 'e made a snatch to unsling 'is rifle. Then 'e cuts 'is hand away saying: "No! Don't tempt me, Bella. We've all Eternity ahead of us. An hour or two won't make any odds." Then he picks up the braziers an' goes on to the dug-out door. He'd finished with me. He pours petrol on 'em, an' lights it with a match, an' carries 'em inside, flarin'. All that time Auntie Armine stood with 'er arms out—an' a look in 'er face! *I* didn't know such things was or could be! Then he comes out an' says: "Come in, my dear"; an' she stoops an' goes into the dug-out with that look on her face—that look on her face! An' then 'e shuts the door from inside an' starts wedgin' it up. So 'elp me Gawd, I saw an' 'eard all these things with my own eyes an' ears!'

He repeated his oath several times. After a long pause Keede asked him if he recalled what happened next.

'It was a bit of a mix-up, for me, from then on. I must have carried on—they told me I did, but—but I was—I felt a—a long way inside of meself, like—if you've ever had that feelin'. I wasn't rightly on the spot at all. They woke me up sometime next morning, because 'e 'adn't showed up at the train; an' some one had seen him with me. I wasn't 'alf cross-examined by all an' sundry till dinner-time.

'Then, I think, I volunteered for Dearlove, who 'ad a sore toe, for a front-line message. I had to keep movin', you see, because I hadn't anything to hold *on* to. Whilst up there, Grant informed me how he'd found Uncle John with the door wedged an' sand-bags stuffed in the cracks. I hadn't waited for that. The knockin' when 'e wedged up was enough for me. 'Like Dad's coffin.'

'No one told *me* the door had been wedged.' Keede spoke severely.

'No need to black a dead man's name, sir.'

'What made Grant go to Butcher's Row?'

'Because he'd noticed Uncle John had been pinchin' charcoal for a week past an' layin' it up behind the old barricade there. So when the 'unt began, he went that way straight as a string, an' when he saw the door shut, he knew. He told me he picked the sand-bags out of the cracks an' shoved 'is hand through and shifted the wedges before any one come along. It looked all right. You said yourself, sir, the door must 'ave blown to.'

'Grant knew what Godsoe meant, then?' Keede snapped.

'Grant knew Godsoe was for it; an' nothin' earthly could 'elp or 'inder. He told me so.'

'And then what did you do?'

'I expect I must 'ave kept on carryin' on, till Headquarters give me that wire from Ma—about Auntie Armine dyin'.'

'When had your Aunt died?'

'On the mornin' of the twenty-first. The mornin' of the 21st! That tore it, d'ye see? As long as I could think, I had kep' tellin' myself it was like those things you lectured about at Arras when we was billeted in the cellars—the Angels of Mons, and so on. But that wire tore it.'

'Oh! Hallucinations! I remember. And that wire tore it?' said Keede.

'Yes! You see'—he half lifted himself off the sofa—''there wasn't a single gor-dam thing left abidin' for me to take hold of, here or hereafter. If the dead *do* rise—and I saw 'em—why why, *anything* can 'appen. Don't you understand?'

He was on his feet now, gesticulating stiffly.

'For I saw 'er,' he repeated. 'I saw 'im an' 'er—she dead since mornin' time, an' he killin' 'imself before my livin' eyes so's to carry on with 'er for all Eternity—an' she 'oldin' out 'er arms for it! I want to know where I'm *at!* Look 'ere, you two—why stand *we* in jeopardy every hour?'

'God knows,' said Keede to himself.

'Hadn't we better ring for some one?' I suggested. 'He'll go off the handle in a second.'

'No, he won't. It's the last kick-up before it takes hold. I know how the stuff works. Hul-lo!'

Strangwick, his hands behind his back and his eyes set, gave tongue in the strained, cracked voice of a boy reciting. 'Not twice in the world shall the Gods do thus,' he cried again and again.

'And I'm damned if it's goin' to be even once for me!' he went on with sudden insane fury. '*I* don't care whether we *'ave* been pricin' things in the windows . . . . *Let* 'er sue if she likes! She don't know what reel things mean. *I* do—I've 'ad occasion to notice 'em . . . . *No*, I tell you! I'll 'ave 'em when I want 'em, an' be done with 'em; but not till I see that look on a face . . . that look. . . . I'm not takin' any. The reel thing's life an' death. It *begins* at death, d'ye see. *She* can't understand . . . . Oh, go on an' push off to Hell, you an' your lawyers. I'm fed up with it—fed up!'

He stopped as abruptly as he had started, and the drawn face broke back to its natural irresolute lines. Keede, holding both his hands, led him back to the sofa, where he dropped like a wet towel, took out some flamboyant robe from a press, and drew it neatly over him.

'Ye-es. *That's* the real thing at last,' said Keede. 'Now he's got it off his mind he'll sleep. By the way, who introduced him?'

'Shall I go and find out?' I suggested.

'Yes; and you might ask him to come here. There's no need for us to stand to all night.'

So I went to the Banquet, which was in full swing, and was seized by an elderly, precise Brother from a South London Lodge, who followed me, concerned and apologetic. Keede soon put him at his ease.

'The boy's had trouble,' our visitor explained. 'I'm most mortified he should have performed his bad turn here. I thought he'd put it be'ind him.'

'I expect talking about old days with me brought it all back,' said Keede. 'It does sometimes.'

'Maybe! Maybe! But over and above that, Clem's had post-war trouble, too.'

'Can't he get a job? He oughtn't to let that weigh on him, at his time of life,' said Keede cheerily.

"'Tisn't that—he's provided for—but '—he coughed confidentially behind his dry hand—'as a matter of fact, Worshipful Sir, he's—he's implicated for the present in a little breach of promise action.'

'Ah! That's a different thing,' said Keede.

'Yes. That's his reel trouble. No reason given, you understand. The young lady in every way suitable, an' she'd make him a good little wife too, if I'm any judge. But he says she ain't his ideel or something. 'No getting at what's in young people's minds these days, is there?'

'I'm afraid there isn't,' said Keede. 'But he's all right now. He'll sleep. You sit by him, and when he wakes, take him home quietly . . . . Oh, we're used to men getting a little upset here. You've nothing to thank us for, Brother—Brother——'

'Armine,' said the old gentleman. 'He's my nephew by marriage.'

'That's all that's wanted!' said Keede.

Brother Armine looked a little puzzled. Keede hastened to explain. 'As I was saying, all he wants now is to be kept quiet till he wakes.'

A FRIEND OF THE FAMILY

There had been rather a long sitting at Lodge 'Faith and Works,' 5837 E.C., that warm April night. Three initiations and two raisings, each conducted with the spaciousness and particularity that our Lodge prides itself upon, made the Brethren a little silent, and the strains of certain music had not yet lifted from them.

'There are two pieces that ought to be barred forever,' said a Brother as we were sitting down to the 'banquet.' '"Last Post" is the other.'

'I can just stand "Last Post." It's "Tipperary" breaks me,' another replied. 'But I expect every one carries his own firing-irons inside him.'

I turned to look. It was a sponsor for one of our newly raised Brethren—a fat man with a fish-like and vacant face, but evidently prosperous. We introduced ourselves as we took our places. His name was Bevin, and he had a chicken farm near Chalfont St. Giles, whence he supplied, on yearly contract, two or three high-class London hotels. He was also, he said, on the edge of launching out into herb-growing.

'There's a demand for herbs,' said he; 'but it all depends upon your connections with the wholesale dealers. *We* ain't systematic enough. The French do it much better, especially in those mountains on the Swiss an' Italian sides. They use more herbal remedies than we do. Our patent-medicine business has killed that with us. But there's a demand still, if your connections are sound. I'm going in for it.'

A large, well-groomed Brother across the table (his name was Pole, and he seemed some sort of professional man) struck in with a detailed account of a hollow behind a destroyed village near Thiepval, where, for no ascertainable reason, a certain rather scarce herb had sprung up by the acre, he said, out of the overturned earth.

'Only you've got to poke among the weeds to find it, and there's any quantity of bombs an' stuff knockin' about there still. They haven't cleaned it up yet.'

'Last time *I* saw the place,' said Bevin, 'I thought it 'ud be that way till Judgment Day. You know how it lay in that dip under that beet-factory. I saw it bombed up level in two days—into brick-dust mainly. They were huntin' for St. Firmin Dump.' He took a sandwich and munched slowly, wiping his face, for the night was close.

'Ye-es,' said Pole. 'The trouble is there hasn't been any judgment taken or executed. That's why the world is where it is now. We didn't need anything but justice—afterwards. Not gettin' that, the bottom fell out of things, naturally.'

'That's how I look at it too,' Bevin replied. 'We didn't want all that talk afterwards—we only wanted justice. What *I* say is, there *must* be a right and a wrong to things. It can't all be kiss-an'-make-friends, no matter what you do.'

A thin, dark brother on my left, who had been attending to a cold pork pie (there are no pork pies to equal ours, which are home-made), suddenly lifted his long head, in which a pale blue glass eye swiveled insanely.

'Well,' he said slowly. '*My* motto is "Never again." Ne-ver again for me.'

'Same here—till next time,' said Pole, across the table. 'You're from Sydney, ain't you?'

'How d'you know?' was the short answer

'You spoke.' The other smiled. So did Bevin, who added: '*I* know how your push talk, well enough. Have you started that Republic of yours down under yet?'

'No. But we're goin' to. *Then* you'll see.'

'Carry on. No one's hindering,' Bevin pursued.

The Australian scowled. 'No. We know they ain't. And—and—that's what makes us all so crazy angry with you.' He threw back his head and laughed the spleen out of him. 'What *can* you do with an Empire that—that don't care what you do?'

'I've heard that before,' Bevin laughed, and his fat sides shook. 'Oh, I know *your* push inside-out.' .

'When did you come across us? My name's Orton—no relation to the Tichborne one.'

'Gallip'li—dead mostly. My battalion began there. We only lost half.'

'Lucky! They gambled *us* away in two days. 'Member the hospital on the beach?' asked asked Orton.

'Yes. An' the man without the face—preaching,' said Bevin, sitting up a little.

'Till he died,' said the Australian, his voice lowered.

'*And* afterwards,' Bevin added, lower still.

'Christ! Were you there that night?'

Bevin nodded. The Australian choked off something he was going to say, as a Brother on his left claimed him. I heard them talk horses, while Bevin developed his herb-growing projects with the well-groomed Brother opposite.

At the end of the banquet, when pipes were drawn, the Australian addressed himself to Bevin, across me, and as the company re-arranged itself, we three came to anchor in the big anteroom where the best prints are hung. Here our Brother across the table joined us, and moored alongside.

The Australian was full of racial grievances, as must be in a young country; alternating between complaints that his people had not been appreciated enough in England, or too fulsomely complimented by an hysterical Press.

'No-o,' Pole drawled, after a while. 'You're altogether wrong. We hadn't time to notice anything—we were all too busy fightin' for our lives. What *your* crowd down under are suffering from is growing-pains. You'll get over 'em in three hundred years or so—if you're allowed to last so long.'

'Who's going to stoush us?' Orton asked fiercely.

This turned the talk again to larger issues and possibilities— delivered on both sides straight from the shoulder without malice or heat, between bursts of song from round the piano at the far end. Bevin and I sat out, watching.

'Well, *I* don't understand these matters,' said Bevin at last. 'But I'd hate to have one of your crowd have it in for me for anything.'

'Would you? Why?' Orton pierced him with his pale, artificial eye.

'Well, you're a trifle—what's the word?—vindictive?—spiteful? At least, that's what *I've* found. I expect it comes from drinking stewed tea with your meat four times a day,' said Bevin. 'No! I'd hate to have an Australian after me for anything in particular.'

Out of this came his tale—somewhat in this shape:

It opened with an Australian of the name of Hickmot or Hickmer—Bevin called him both—who, finding his battalion completely expended at Gallipoli, had joined up with what stood of Bevin's battalion, and had there remained, unrebuked and unnoticed. The point that Bevin laboured was that his man had never seen a table-cloth, a china plate, or a dozen white people together till, in his thirtieth year, he had walked for two months to Brisbane to join up. Pole found this hard to believe.

'But it's true,' Bevin insisted. 'This chap was born an' bred among the black fellers, as they call 'em, two hundred miles from the nearest town, four hundred miles from a railway, an' ten thousand from the grace o' God—out in Queensland near some desert.'

'Why, of course. We come out of everywhere,' said Orton. 'What's wrong with that?'

'Yes—but—— Look here! From the time that this man Hickmot was twelve years old he'd ridden, driven—what's the word?—conducted sheep for his father for thousands of miles on end, an' months at a time, alone with these black fellers that you daren't show the back of your neck to—else they knock your head in. That was all that he'd ever done till he joined up. He—he—didn't *belong* to anything m the world, you understand. And he didn't strike other men as being a—a human being.'

'Why? He was a Queensland drover. They're all right,' Orton explained.

'I dare say; but—well, a man notices another man, don't he? You'd notice if there was a man standing or sitting or lyin' near you, wouldn't you? So'd any one. But you'd never notice Hickmot. His bein' anywhere about wouldn't stay in your mind. He just didn't draw attention any more than anything else that happened to be about. Have you got it?'

'Wasn't he any use at his job?' Pole inquired.

'I've nothing against him that way, an' I'm—I was his platoon sergeant. He wouldn't volunteer specially for any doings, but he'd slip out with the party and he'd slip back with what was left of 'em. No one noticed him, and he never opened his mouth about any doings. You'd think a man who had lived the way he'd lived among black fellers an' sheep would be noticeable enough in an English battalion, wouldn't you?'

'It teaches 'em to lie close; but *you* seem to have noticed him,' Orton interposed, with a little suspicion.

'Not at the time—but afterwards. If he was noticeable it was on account of his *un*noticeability—same way you'd notice there not being an extra step at the bottom of the staircase when you thought there was.'

'Ye-es,' Pole said suddenly. 'It's the eternal mystery of personality. "God before Whom ever lie bare——" Some people can occlude their personality like turning off a tap. I beg your pardon. Carry on!'

'Granted,' said Bevin. 'I think I catch your drift. I used to think I was a student of human nature before I joined up.'

'What was your job—before?' Orton asked.

'Oh, I was *the* young blood of the village. Goal-keeper in our soccer team, secretary of the local cricket and rifle—oh, lor'!—clubs. Yes, an' village theatricals. My father was the chemist in the village. *How* I did talk! *What* I did know!' He beamed upon us all.

'*I* don't mind hearing you talk,' said Orton, lying back in his chair. 'You're a little different from some of 'em. What happened to this dam' drover of yours?'

'He was with our push for the rest of the war—an' I don't think he ever sprung a dozen words at one time. With his upbringing, you see, there wasn't any subject that any man knew about he *could* open up on. He kept quiet, and mixed with his backgrounds. If there was a lump of dirt, or a hole in the ground, or what was—was left after anythin' had happened, it would be Hickmot. That was all he wanted to be.'

'A camouflager?' Orton suggested.

'You have it! He was the complete camouflager all through. That's him to a dot. Look here! He hadn't even a nickname in his platoon! And then a friend of mine from our village, of the name of Vigors, came out with a draft. Bert Vigors. As a matter of fact, I was engaged to his sister. And Bert hadn't been with us a week before they called him "The Grief." His father was an oldish man, a market-gardener—high-class vegetables, bit o' glass, an'—an' all the rest of it. Do you know anything about that particular business?'

'Not much, I'm afraid,' said Pole, 'except that glass is expensive, and one's man always sells the cut flowers.'

'Then you do know something about it. It is. Bert was the old man's only son, an'—*I* don't blame him—he'd done his damnedest to get exempted—for the sake of the business, you understand. But he caught it all right. The tribunal wasn't takin' any the day he went up. Bert was for it, with a few remarks from the patriotic old was-sers on the bench. Our county paper had 'em all.'

'That's the thing that made one really want the Hun in England for a week or two,' said Pole.

'*Mwor osee!* The same tribunal, havin' copped Bert, gave unconditional exemption to the opposition shop—a man called Margetts, in the market-garden business, which he'd established *since* the war, with his two sons who, every one in the village knew, had been pushed into the business to save their damned hides. But Margetts had a good lawyer to advise him. The whole case was frank and above-board to a degree—our county paper had it all in, too. Agricultural producevital necessity; the plough mightier than the sword; an' those ducks on the bench, who had turned down Bert, noddin' and smilin' at Margetts, all full of his cabbage and green peas. What happened? The usual. Vigors' business—he's sixty-eight, with asthma—goes smash, and Margetts and Co. double theirs. So, then, that was Bert's grievance, an' he joined us full of it. That's why they called him "The Grief." Knowing the facts, I was with him; but being his sergeant, I had to check him, because grievances are catchin', and three or four men with 'em make Companies—er—sticky. Luckily Bert wasn't handy with his pen. He had to cork up his grievance mostly till he came across Hickmot, an' Gord in Heaven knows what brought those two together. No! *As* y'were. I'm wrong about God! I always am. It was Sheep. Bert knew's much about sheep as I do—an' that's Canterbury lamb—but he'd let Hickmot talk about 'em for hours, in return for Hickmot listenin' to his grievance. Hickmot 'ud talk sheep—the one created thing he'd ever open up on—an' Bert 'ud talk his grievance while they was waiting to go over the top. I've heard 'em again an' again, and, of course, I encouraged 'em. Now, look here! Hickmot hadn't seen an English house or a field or a road or—or anything any civ'lised man is used to in all his life! Sheep an' blacks! Market-gardens an' glass an' exemption-tribunals! An' the men's teeth chatterin' behind their masks between rum-issue an' zero. Oh, there was fun in Hell those days, wasn't there, boys?'

'Sure! Oh, sure!' Orton chuckled, and Pole echoed him.

'Look here! When we were lying up somewhere among those forsaken chicken-camps back o' Doullens, I found Hickmot making mud-pies in a farmyard an' Bert lookin' on. He'd made a model of our village according to Bert's description of it. He'd preserved it in his head through all those weeks an' weeks o' Bert's yap; an' he'd coughed it all up—Margetts' house and gardens, old Mr. Vigors' ditto; both pubs; my father's shop, everything that he'd been told by Bert done out to scale in mud, with bits o' brick and stick. Haig ought to have seen it; but as his sergeant I had to check him for misusin' his winkle-pin on dirt. 'Come to think of it, a man who runs about uninhabited countries, with sheep, for a livin' must have gifts for mappin' and scalin' things somehow or other, or he'd be dead. *I* never saw anything like it—*all* out o' what Bert had told him by word of mouth. An' the next time we went up the line Hickmot copped it in the leg just in front of me.'

'Finish?' I asked.

'Oh, no. Only beginnin'. That was in December, somethin' or other, '16. In Jan'ry Vigors copped it for keeps. I buried him—snowin' blind it was—an' before we'd got him under the whole show was crumped. I wanted to bury him again just to spite 'em (I'm a spiteful man by nature), but the party wasn't takin' any more—even if they could have found it. But, you see, we had buried him all right, which is what they want at home, and I wrote the usual trimmin's about the chaplain an' the full service, an' what his captain had said about Bert bein' recommended for a pip, an' the irreparable loss an' so on. That was in Jan'ry '17. In Feb'ry some time or other I got saved. My speciality had come to be bombin's and night-doings. Very pleasant for a young free man, but—there's a limit to what you can stand. It takes all men differently. Noise was what started me, at last. I'd got just up to the edge—wonderin' when I'd crack an' how many of our men I'd do in if it came on me while we were busy. I had that nice taste in the mouth and the nice temperature they call trench-fever, an'—I had to feel inside my head for the meanin' of every order I gave or was responsible for executin'. *You* know!'

'We do. Go on!' said Pole in a tone that made Orton look at him.

'So, you see, the bettin' was even on my drawin' a V.C. or getting Number Umpty rest-camp or—a firing party before breakfast. But Gord saved me. (I made friends with Him the last two years of the war. The others went off too quick.) They wanted a bomb in'-instructor for the training-battalion at home, an' He put it into their silly hearts to indent for me. It took 'em five minutes to make me understand I was saved. Then I vomited, an' then I cried. *You* know!' The fat face of Bevin had changed and grown drawn, even as he spoke; and his hands tugged as though to tighten an imaginary belt.

'I was never keen on bombin' myself,' said Pole. 'But bomb in'-instruction's murder!'

'I don't deny it's a shade risky, specially when they take the pin out an' start shakin' it, same as the Chinks used to do in the woods at Beauty, when they were cuttin' 'em down. But you live like a home defence Brigadier, besides week-end leaf. As a matter o' fact, I married Bert's sister soon's I could after I got the billet, an' I used to lie in our bed thinkin' of the old crowd on the Somme an'—feelin' what a swine I was. Of course, I earned two V.C.'s a week behind the traverse in the exercise of my ord'nary duties, but that isn't the same thing. An' yet I'd only joined up because—because I couldn't dam' well help it.'

'An' what about your Queenslander?' the Australian asked.

'*Too de sweet! Pronto!* We got a letter in May from a Brighton hospital matron, sayin' that one of the name of Hickmer was anxious for news o' me, previous to proceedin' to Roehampton for initiation into his new leg. Of course, we applied for him by return. Bert had written about him to his sister—my missus—every time he wrote at all; an' any pal o' Bert's—well, *you* know what the ladies are like. I warned her about his peculiarities. She wouldn't believe till she saw him. He was just the same. You'd ha' thought he'd show up in England like a fresh stiff on snow—but you never noticed him. You never heard him; and if he didn't want to be seen he wasn't there. He just joined up with his background. I knew he could do that with men; but how in Hell, seein' how curious women are, he could camouflage with the ladies—my wife an' my mother to wit—beats *me*! He'd feed the chickens for us; he'd stand on his one leg—it was off above the knee—and saw wood for us. He'd run—I mean he'd hop—errands for Mrs. B, or mother; our dog worshipped him from the start, though I never saw him throw a word to him; and—*yet* he didn't take any place anywhere. You've seen a rabbit—you've seen a pheasant—hidin' in a ditch? 'Put your hand on it sometimes before it moved, haven't you? Well, that was Hickmot—with two women in the house crazy to find out—find out—anything about him that made him human. *You* know what women are! He stayed with us a fortnight. He left us on a Sat'day to go to Roehampton to try his leg. On Friday he came over to the bombin' ground—not saym' anything, *as* usual—to watch me instruct my Suicide Club, which was only half an hour's run by rail from our village. He had his overcoat on, an' as soon as he reached the place it was *mafeesh* with him, as usual. Rabbit-trick again! You never noticed him. He sat in the bomb-proof behind the pit where the duds accumulate till it's time to explode 'em. Naturally, that's strictly forbidden to the public. So he went there, an' no one noticed him. When he'd had enough of watchin', he hopped off home to feed our chickens for the last time.'

'Then how did *you* know all about it?' Orton said.

'Because I saw him come into the place just as I was goin' down into the trench. Then he slipped my memory till my train went back. But it would have made no difference what our arrangements were. If Hickmer didn't choose to be noticed, he *wasn't* noticed. Just for curiosity's sake I asked some o' the Staff Sergeants whether they'd seen him on the ground. Not one—not one single one had—or could tell me what he was like. An', Sat'day noon, he went off to Roehampton. We saw him into the train ourselves, with the lunch Mrs. B. had put up for him—a one-legged man an' his crutch, in regulation blue, khaki warm an' kit-bag. Takin' everything together, per'aps he'd spoken as many as twenty times in the thirteen days he'd been with us. I'm givin' it you straight as it happened. An' now—look here!—this is what *did* happen.

'Between two and three that Sunday morning—dark an' blowin' from the north—I was woke up by an explosion an' people shoutin' "Raid!" The first bang fetched 'em out like worms after rain. There was another some minutes afterwards, an' me an' a Sergeant in the Shropshires on leaf told 'em all to take cover. They did. There was a devil of a long wait an' there was a third pop. Everybody, includin' me, heard aeroplanes. I didn't notice till afterwards that——'

Bevin paused.

'What?' said Orton.

'Oh, I noticed a heap of things afterwards. What we noticed first—the Shropshire Sergeant an' me—was a rick well alight back o' Margetts' house, an', with that north wind, blowin' straight on to another rick o' Margetts'. It went up all of a whoosh. The next thing we saw by the light of it was Margetts' house with a bomb-hole in the roof and the rafters leanin' sideways like—like they always lean on such occasions. So we ran there, and the first thing we met was Margetts in his split-tailed nightie callin' on his mother an' damnin' his wife. A man always does that when he's cross. Have you noticed? Mrs. Margetts was in her nightie too, remindin' Margetts that he hadn't completed his rick insurance. An' that's a woman's lovin' care all over. Behind them was their eldest son, in trousers an' slippers, nursin' his arm an' callin' for the doctor. They went through us howlin' like *flammemwerfer* casualties—right up the street to the surgery.

'Well, there wasn't anything to do except let the show burn out. We hadn't any means of extinguishing conflagrations. Some of 'em fiddled with buckets, an' some of 'em tried to get out some o' Margetts' sticks, but his younger son kept shoutin', "Don't! Don't! It'll be stole! It'll be stole!" So it burned instead, till the roof came down, top of all—a little, cheap, dirty villa, In *reel* life one whizz-bang would have shifted it; but in our civil village it looked that damned important and particular you wouldn't believe. We couldn't get round to Margetts' stable because of the two ricks alight, but we found some one had opened the door early an' the horses was in Margetts' new vegetable piece down the hill which he'd hired off old Vigors to extend his business with. I love the way a horse always looks after his own belly—same as a Gunner. They went to grazin' down the carrots and onions till young Margetts ran to turn 'em out, an' then they got in among the glass frames an' cut themselves. Oh, we had a regular Russian night of it, everybody givin' advice an' fallin' over each other. When it got light we saw the damage. House, two ricks an' stable *mafeesh*; the big glasshouse with every pane smashed and the furnace-end of it blown clean out. All the horses an' about fifteen head o' cattle—butcher's stores from the next field—feeding in the new vegetable piece. It was a fair clean-up from end to end—house, furniture, fittin's, plant, an' all the early crops.'

'Was there any other damage in the village?' I asked.

'I'm coming to it—the curious part—but I wouldn't call it damage. I was renting a field then for my chickens off the Merecroft Estate. It's accommodation-land, an' there was a wet ditch at the bottom that I had wanted for ever so long to dam up to make a swim-hole for Mrs. Bevin's ducks.'

'Ah!' said Orton, half turning in his chair, all in one piece.

'S'pose I was allowed? Not me. Their Agent came down on me for tamperin' with the Estate's drainage arrangements. An' all I wanted was to bring the bank down where the ditch narrows—a couple of cartloads of dirt would have held the water back for half-a-dozen yards—not more than that, an' I could have made a little spill-way over the top with three boards-same as in trenches. Well, the first bomb—the one that woke me up—had done my work for me better than I could. It had dropped just under the hollow of the bank an' brought it all down in a fair landslide. I'd got my swim-hole for Mrs. Bevin's ducks, an' I didn't see how the Estate could kick at the Act o' God, d'you?'

'And Hickmot?' said Orton, grinning.

'Hold on! There was a Parish Council meetin' to demand reprisals, of course, an' there was the policeman an' me pokin' about among the ruins till the Explosives Expert came down in his motor car at three p.m. Monday, an' he meets all the Margetts off their rockers, howlin' in the surgery, an' he sees my swim-hole fillin' up to the brim.'

'What did he say?' Pole inquired.

'He sized it up at once. (He had to get back to dine in town that evening.) He said all the evidence proved that it was a lucky shot on the part of one isolated Hun 'plane gom' home, an' we weren't to take it to heart. I don't know that anybody but the Margetts did. He said they must have used incendiary bombs of a new type—which he'd suspected for a long time. I don't think the man was any worse than God intended him to be. I don't *reelly*. But the Shropshire Sergeant said——'

'And what did *you* think?' I interrupted.

'I didn't think. I knew by then. I'm not a Sherlock Holmes; but havin' chucked 'em an' chucked 'em back and kicked 'em out of the light an' slept with 'em for two years, an' makin' my livin' out of them at that time, I could recognise the fuse of a Mills bomb when I found it. I found all three of 'em. 'Curious about that second in Margetts' glasshouse. Hickmot mus' have raked the ashes out of the furnace, popped it in, an' shut the furnace door. It operated all right. Not one livin' pane left in the putty, and all the brickwork spread round the yard in streaks. Just like that St. Firmin village we were talking about.'

'But how d'you account for young what's—hisname gettin' his arm broken?' said Pole.

'Crutch!' said Bevin. 'If you or me had taken on that night's doin's, with one leg, we'd have hopped and sweated from one flank to another an' been caught half-way between. Hickmot didn't. I'm as sure as I'm sittin' here that he did his doings quiet and comfortable at his full height— he was over six feet—and no one noticed him. This is the way *I* see it. He fixed the swim-hole for Mrs. Bevin's ducks first. We used to talk over our own affairs in front of him, of course, and he knew just what she wanted in the way of a pond. So he went and made it at his leisure. Then he prob'ly went over to Margetts' and lit the first rack, knowin' that the wind 'ud do the rest. When young Margetts saw the light of it an' came out to look, Hickmot would have taken post at the back-door an' dropped the young swine with his crutch, same as we used to drop Huns comin' out of a dug-out. *You* know how they blink at the light? Then he must have walked off an' opened Margetts' stable door to save the horses. They'd be more to him than any man's life. Then he prob'ly chucked one bomb on top o' Margetts' roof, havin' seen that the first rick had caught the second and that the whole house was bound to go. D'you get me?'

'Then why did he waste his bomb on the house?' said Orton. His glass eye seemed as triumphant as his real one.

'For camouflage, of course. He was camouflagin' an air-raid. When the Margetts piled out of their place into the street, he prob'ly attended to the glasshouse, because that would be Margetts' chief means o' business. After that—I think so, because otherwise I don't see where all those extra cattle came from that we found in the vegetable piece—he must have walked off an' rounded up all the butcher's beasts in the next medder, an' driven 'em there to help the horses. And when he'd finished everything he'd set out to do, I'll lay my life an' kit he curled up like a bloomin' wombat not fifty yards away from the whole flamin' show—an' let us run round him. An' when he'd had his sleep out, he went up to Roehampton Monday mornin' by some tram that he'd decided upon in his own mind weeks an' weeks before.'

'Did he know all the trains then?' said Pole.

'Ask me another. I only know that if he wanted to get from any place to another without bein' noticed, he did it.'

'And the bombs? He got 'em from you, of course,' Pole went on.

'What do *you* think? He was an hour in the park watchin' me instruct, sittin', as I remember, in the bomb-proof by the dud-hole, in his overcoat. He got 'em all right. He took neither more nor less than he wanted; an' I've told you what he did with 'em—one—two—*an'* three.'

"Ever see him afterwards?' said Orton.

'Yes. 'Saw him at Brighton when I went down there with the missus, not a month after he'd been broken in to his Roehampton leg. You know how the boys used to sit all along Brighton front in their blues, an' jump every time the coal was bein' delivered to the hotels behind them? I barged into him opposite the Old Ship, an' I told him about our air-raid. I told him how Margetts had gone off his rocker an' walked about starin' at the sky an' holdin' reprisal-meetin's all by himself; an' how old Mr. Vigors had bought in what he'd left—tho' of course I said what *was* left—o' Margetts' business; an' how well my swim-hole for the ducks was doin'. It didn't interest him. He didn't want to come over to stay with us any more, either. We were a long, long way back in his past. You could see that. He wanted to get back with his new leg, to his own God-forsaken sheep-walk an' his black fellers in Queensland. I expect he's done it now, an' no one has noticed him. But, by Gord! He *did* leak a little at the end. He did that much! When we was waitin' for the tram to the station, I said how grateful I was to Fritz for moppin' up Margetts an' makin' our swim-hole all in one night. Mrs. B. seconded the motion. We couldn't have done less. Well, then Hickmot said, speakin' in his queer way, as if English words were all new to him: "Ah, go on an' bail up in Hell," he says. "Bert was my friend." That was all. I've given it you just as it happened, word for word. I'd hate to have an Australian have it in for *me* for anything I'd done to *his* friend. Mark you, I don't say there's anything *wrong* with you Australians, Brother Orton. I only say they ain't like us or any one else that I know.'

'Well, do you want us to be?' said Orton.

'No, no. It takes all sorts to make a world, as the sayin' is. And now'—Bevin pulled out his gold watch—'if I don't make a move of it I'll miss my last train.'

'Let her go,' said Orton serenely. 'You've done some lorry-hoppin' in your time, haven't you—Sergeant?'

'When I was two an' a half stone lighter, Digger,' Bevin smiled in reply.

'Well, I'll run you out home before sun-up. I'm a haulage-contractor now—London and Oxford. There's an empty of mine ordered to Oxford. We can go round by your place as easy as not. She's lyin' out Vauxhall-way.'

'My Gord ! An' see the sun rise again! 'Haven't seen him since I can't remember when,' said Bevin, chuckling. 'Oh, there was fun sometimes in Hell, wasn't there, Australia?'; and again his hands event down to tighten the belt that was missing.

THE MAN WHO WOULD BE KING

"Brother to a Prince and fellow to a beggar if he be found worthy."

The Law, as quoted, lays down a fair conduct of life, and one not easy to follow. I have been fellow to a beggar again and again under circumstances which prevented either of us finding out whether the other was worthy. I have still to be brother to a Prince, though I once came near to kinship with what might have been a veritable King and was promised the reversion of a Kingdom — army, law-courts, revenue and policy all complete. But, to-day, I greatly fear that my King is dead, and if I want a crown I must go and hunt it for myself.

The beginning of everything was in a railway train upon the road to Mhow from Ajmir. There had been a deficit in the Budget, which necessitated travelling, not Second-class, which is only half as dear as First-class, but by Intermediate, which is very awful indeed. There are no cushions in the Intermediate class, and the population are either Intermediate, which is Eurasian, or native, which for a long night journey is nasty; or Loafer, which is amusing though intoxicated. Intermediates do not patronize refreshment-rooms. They carry their food in bundles and pots, and buy sweets from the native sweetmeat-sellers, and drink the roadside water. That is why in the hot weather Intermediates are taken out of the carriages dead, and in all weathers are most properly looked down upon.

My particular Intermediate happened to be empty till I reached Nasirabad, when a huge gentleman in shirt-sleeves entered, and, following the custom of Intermediates, passed the time of day. He was a wanderer and a vagabond like myself, but with an educated taste for whiskey. He told tales of things he had seen and done, of out-of-the-way corners of the Empire into which he had penetrated, and of adventures in which he risked his life for a few days' food. "If India was filled with men like you and me, not knowing more than the crows where they'd get their next day's rations, it isn't seventy millions of revenue the land would be paying

— it's seven hundred million," said he; and as I looked at his mouth and chin I was disposed to agree with him. We talked politics — the politics of Loaferdom that sees things from the underside where the lath and plaster is not smoothed off — and we talked postal arrangements because my friend wanted to send a telegram back from the next station to Ajmir, which is the turning-off place from the Bombay to the Mhow line as you travel westward. My friend had no money beyond eight annas which he wanted for dinner, and I had no money at all, owing to the hitch in the Budget before mentioned. Further, I was going into a wilderness where, though I should resume touch with the Treasury, there were no telegraph offices. I was, therefore, unable to help him in any way.

"We might threaten a Station-master, and make him send a wire on tick," said my friend, "but that'd mean inquiries for you and for me, and I've got my hands full these days. Did you say you are travelling back along this line within any days?"

"Within ten," I said.

"Can't you make it eight?" said he. "Mine is rather urgent business."

"I can send your telegram within ten days if that will serve you," I said.

"I couldn't trust the wire to fetch him now I think of it. It's this way. He leaves Delhi on the 23d for Bombay. That means he'll be running through Ajmir about the night of the 23d."

"But I'm going into the Indian Desert," I explained.

"Well *and* good," said he. "You'll be changing at Marwar Junction to get into Jodhpore territory — you must do that — and he'll be coming through Marwar Junction in the early morning of the 24th by the Bombay Mail. Can you be at Marwar Junction on that time? 'Twon't be inconveniencing you because I know that there's precious few pickings to be got out of these Central India States — even though you pretend to be correspondent of the *Backwoodsman*."

94

"Have you ever tried that trick?" I asked.

"Again and again, but the Residents find you out, and then you get escorted to the Border before you've time to get your knife into them. But about my friend here. I *must* give him a word o' mouth to tell him what's come to me or else he won't know where to go. I would take it more than kind of you if you was to come out of Central India in time to catch him at Marwar Junction, and say to him:— 'He has gone South for the week.' He'll know what that means. He's a big man with a red beard, and a great swell he is. You'll find him sleeping like a gentleman with all his luggage round him in a second-class compartment. But don't you be afraid. Slip down the window, and say:— 'He has gone South for the week,' and he'll tumble. It's only cutting your time of stay in those parts by two days. I ask you as a stranger — going to the West," he said with emphasis.

"Where have *you* come from?" said I.

"From the East," said he, "and I am hoping that you will give him the message on the Square — for the sake of my Mother as well as your own."

Englishmen are not usually softened by appeals to the memory of their mothers, but for certain reasons, which will be fully apparent, I saw fit to agree.

"It's more than a little matter," said he, "and that's why I ask you to do it — and now I know that I can depend on you doing it. A second-class carriage at Marwar Junction, and a red-haired man asleep in it. You'll be sure to remember. I get out at the next station, and I must hold on there till he comes or sends me what I want."

"I'll give the message if I catch him," I said, "and for the sake of your Mother as well as mine I'll give you a word of advice. Don't try to run the Central India States just now as the correspondent of the *Backwoodsman*. There's a real one knocking about here, and it might lead to trouble."

"Thank you," said he simply, "and when will the swine be gone? I can't starve because he's ruining my work. I wanted to get hold of the Degumber Rajah down here about his father's widow, and give him a jump."

"What did he do to his father's widow, then?"

"Filled her up with red pepper and slippered her to death as she hung from a beam. I found that out myself and I'm the only man that would dare going into the State to get hush-money for it. They'll try to poison me, same as they did in Chortumna when I went on the loot there. But you'll give the man at Marwar Junction my message?"

He got out at a little roadside station, and I reflected. I had heard, more than once, of men personating correspondents of newspapers and bleeding small Native States with threats of exposure, but I had never met any of the caste before. They lead a hard life, and generally die with great suddenness. The Native States have a wholesome horror of English newspapers, which may throw light on their peculiar methods of government, and do their best to choke correspondents with champagne, or drive them out of their mind with four-in-hand barouches. They do not understand that nobody cares a straw for the internal administration of Native States so long as oppression and crime are kept within decent limits, and the ruler is not drugged, drunk, or diseased from one end of the year to the other. Native States were created by Providence in order to supply picturesque scenery, tigers and tall-writing. They are the dark places of the earth, full of unimaginable cruelty, touching the Railway and the Telegraph on one side, and, on the other, the days of Harun-al-Raschid. When I left the train I did business with divers Kings, and in eight days passed through many changes of life. Sometimes I wore dress-clothes and consorted with Princes and Politicals, drinking from crystal and eating from silver. Sometimes I lay out upon the ground and devoured what I could get, from a plate made of a flapjack, and drank the running water, and slept under the same rug as my servant. It was all in a day's work.

Then I headed for the Great Indian Desert upon the proper date, as I had promised, and the night Mail set me down at Marwar Junction, where a funny little, happy-go-lucky, native managed railway runs to Jodhpore. The Bombay Mail from Delhi makes a short halt at Marwar. She arrived as I got in, and I had just time to hurry to her platform and go down the carriages. There was only one second-class on the train. I slipped the window and looked down upon a flaming red beard, half covered by a railway rug. That was my man, fast asleep, and I dug him gently in the ribs. He woke with a grunt and I saw his face in the light of the lamps. It was a great and shining face.

"Tickets again?" said he.

"No," said I. "I am to tell you that he is gone South for the week. He is gone South for the week!"

The train had begun to move out. The red man rubbed his eyes. "He has gone South for the week," he repeated. "Now that's just like his impudence. Did he say that I was to give you anything? — 'Cause I won't."

"He didn't," I said and dropped away, and watched the red lights die out in the dark. It was horribly cold because the wind was blowing off the sands. I climbed into my own train — not an Intermediate Carriage this time — and went to sleep.

If the man with the beard had given me a rupee I should have kept it as a memento of a rather curious affair. But the consciousness of having done my duty was my only reward.

Later on I reflected that two gentlemen like my friends could not do any good if they foregathered and personated correspondents of newspapers, and might, if they "stuck up" one of the little rat-trap states of Central India or Southern Rajputana, get themselves into serious difficulties. I therefore took some trouble to describe them as accurately as I could remember to people who would be interested in deporting them; and succeeded, so I was later informed, in having them headed back from the Degumber borders.

Then I became respectable, and returned to an Office where there were no Kings and no incidents except the daily manufacture of a newspaper. A newspaper office seems to attract every conceivable sort of person, to the prejudice of discipline. Zenana-mission ladies arrive, and beg that the Editor will instantly abandon all his duties to describe a Christian prize-giving in a back-slum of a perfectly inaccessible village; Colonels who have been overpassed for commands sit down and sketch the outline of a series of ten, twelve, or twenty-four leading articles on Seniority *versus* Selection; missionaries wish to know why they have not been permitted to escape from their regular vehicles of abuse and swear at a brother-missionary under special patronage of the editorial We; stranded theatrical companies troop up to explain that they cannot pay for their advertisements, but on their return from New Zealand or Tahiti will do so with interest; inventors of patent punkah-pulling machines, carriage couplings and unbreakable swords and axle-trees call with specifications in their pockets and hours at their disposal; tea-companies enter and elaborate their prospectuses with the office pens; secretaries of ball-committees clamor to have the glories of their last dance more fully expounded; strange ladies rustle in and say:— "I want a hundred lady's cards printed *at once*, please," which is manifestly part of an Editor's duty; and every dissolute ruffian that ever tramped the Grand Trunk Road makes it his business to ask for employment as a proof-reader. And, all the time, the telephone-bell is ringing madly, and Kings are being killed on the Continent, and Empires are saying, "You're another," and Mister Gladstone is calling down brimstone upon the British Dominions, and the little black copy-boys are whining, "*kaa-pi chayha-yeh*" (copy wanted) like tired bees, and most of the paper is as blank as Modred's shield.

But that is the amusing part of the year. There are other six months wherein none ever come to call, and the thermometer walks inch by inch up to the top of the glass, and the office is darkened to just above reading light, and the press machines are red-hot of touch, and nobody writes anything but accounts of amusements in the Hill-stations or obituary notices. Then the telephone becomes a tinkling terror, because it tells you of the sudden deaths of men and women that you knew intimately, and the prickly-heat covers you as with a garment, and you sit down and write:— "A slight increase of sickness is reported from the Khuda Janta Khan District. The outbreak is purely sporadic in its nature, and, thanks to the energetic efforts of the District authorities, is now almost at an end. It is, however, with deep regret we record the death, etc."

Then the sickness really breaks out, and the less recording and reporting the better for the peace of the subscribers. But the Empires and the Kings continue to divert themselves as selfishly as before, and the foreman thinks that a daily paper really ought to come out once in twenty-four hours, and all the people at the Hill-stations in the middle of their amusements say:— "Good gracious! Why can't the paper be sparkling? I'm sure there's plenty going on up here."

That is the dark half of the moon, and, as the advertisements say, "must be experienced to be appreciated."

It was in that season, and a remarkably evil season, that the paper began running the last issue of the week on Saturday night, which is to say Sunday morning, after the custom of a London paper. This was a great convenience, for immediately after the paper was put to bed, the dawn would lower the thermometer from 96° to almost 84° for almost half an hour, and in that chill — you have no idea how cold is 84° on the grass until you begin to pray for it — a very tired man could set off to sleep ere the heat roused him.

One Saturday night it was my pleasant duty to put the paper to bed alone. A King or courtier or a courtesan or a community was going to die or get a new Constitution, or do something that was important on the other side of the world, and the paper was to be held open till the latest possible minute in order to catch the telegram. It was a pitchy black night, as stifling as a June night can be, and the *loo*, the red-hot wind from the westward, was booming among the tinder-dry trees and pretending that the rain was on its heels. Now and again a spot of almost boiling water would fall on the dust with the flop of a frog, but all our weary world knew that was only pretence. It was a shade cooler in the press-room than the office, so I sat there, while the type ticked and clicked, and the night-jars hooted at the windows, and the all but naked compositors wiped the sweat from their foreheads and called for water. The thing that was keeping us back, whatever it was, would not come off, though the *loo* dropped and the last type was set, and the whole round earth stood still in the choking heat, with its finger on its lip, to wait the event. I drowsed, and wondered whether the telegraph was a blessing, and whether this dying man, or struggling people, was aware of the inconvenience the delay was causing. There was no special reason beyond the heat and worry to make tension, but, as the clock-hands crept up to three o'clock and the machines spun their fly-wheels two and three times to see that all was in order, before I said the word that would set them off, I could have shrieked aloud.

Then the roar and rattle of the wheels shivered the quiet into little bits. I rose to go away, but two men in white clothes stood in front of me. The first one said:— "It's him!" The second said—"So it is!" And they both laughed almost as loudly as the machinery roared, and mopped their foreheads. "We see there was a light burning across the road and we were sleeping in that ditch there for coolness, and I said to my friend here, the office is open. Let's come along and speak to him as turned us back from the Degumber State," said the smaller of the two. He was the man I had met in the Mhow train, and his fellow was the red-bearded man of Marwar Junction. There was no mistaking the eyebrows of the one or the beard of the other.

I was not pleased, because I wished to go to sleep, not to squabble with loafers. "What do you want?" I asked.

"Half an hour's talk with you cool and comfortable, in the office," said the red-bearded man. "We'd *like* some drink — the Contrack doesn't begin yet, Peachey, so you needn't look — but what we really want is advice. We don't want money. We ask you as a favor, because you did us a bad turn about Degumber."

100

I led from the press-room to the stifling office with the maps on the walls, and the red-haired man rubbed his hands. "That's something like," said he. "This was the proper shop to come to. Now, Sir, let me introduce to you Brother Peachey Carnehan, that's him, and Brother Daniel Dravot, that is *me*, and the less said about our professions the better, for we have been most things in our time. Soldier, sailor, compositor, photographer, proof-reader, street-preacher, and correspondents of the *Backwoodsman* when we thought the paper wanted one. Carnehan is sober, and so am I. Look at us first and see that's sure. It will save you cutting into my talk. We'll take one of your cigars apiece, and you shall see us light." I watched the test. The men were absolutely sober, so I gave them each a tepid peg.

"Well *and* good," said Carnehan of the eyebrows, wiping the froth from his mustache. "Let me talk now, Dan. We have been all over India, mostly on foot. We have been boiler-fitters, engine-drivers, petty contractors, and all that, and we have decided that India isn't big enough for such as us."

They certainly were too big for the office. Dravot's beard seemed to fill half the room and Carnehan's shoulders the other half, as they sat on the big table. Carnehan continued: — "The country isn't half worked out because they that governs it won't let you touch it. They spend all their blessed time in governing it, and you can't lift a spade, nor chip a rock, nor look for oil, nor anything like that without all the Government saying — 'Leave it alone and let us govern.' Therefore, such as it is, we will let it alone, and go away to some other place where a man isn't crowded and can come to his own. We are not little men, and there is nothing that we are afraid of except Drink, and we have signed a Contrack on that. *Therefore*, we are going away to be Kings."

"Kings in our own right," muttered Dravot.

"Yes, of course," I said. "You've been tramping in the sun, and it's a very warm night, and hadn't you better sleep over the notion? Come to-morrow."

"Neither drunk nor sunstruck," said Dravot. "We have slept over the notion half a year, and require to see Books and Atlases, and we have decided that there is only one place now in the world that two strong men can Sar-a-*whack*. They call it Kafiristan. By my reckoning its the top right-hand corner of Afghanistan, not more than three hundred miles from Peshawar. They have two and thirty heathen idols there, and we'll be the thirty-third. It's a mountainous country, and the women of those parts are very beautiful."

"But that is provided against in the Contrack," said Carnehan. "Neither Women nor Liquor, Daniel."

"And that's all we know, except that no one has gone there, and they fight, and in any place where they fight a man who knows how to drill men can always be a King. We shall go to those parts and say to any King we find — 'D' you want to vanquish your foes?' and we will show him how to drill men; for that we know better than anything else. Then we will subvert that King and seize his Throne and establish a Dy-nasty."

"You'll be cut to pieces before you're fifty miles across the Border," I said. "You have to travel through Afghanistan to get to that country. It's one mass of mountains and peaks and glaciers, and no Englishman has been through it. The people are utter brutes, and even if you reached them you couldn't do anything."

"That's more like," said Carnehan. "If you could think us a little more mad we would be more pleased. We have come to you to know about this country, to read a book about it, and to be shown maps. We want you to tell us that we are fools and to show us your books." He turned to the book-cases.

"Are you at all in earnest?" I said.

"A little," said Dravot, sweetly. "As big a map as you have got, even if it's all blank where Kafiristan is, and any books you've got. We can read, though we aren't very educated."

I uncased the big thirty-two-miles-to-the-inch map of India, and two smaller Frontier maps, hauled down volume INF-KAN of the *Encyclopædia Britannica*, and the men consulted them.

"See here!" said Dravot, his thumb on the map. "Up to Jagdallak, Peachey and me know the road. We was there with Roberts's Army. We'll have to turn off to the right at Jagdallak through Laghmann territory. Then we get among the hills — fourteen thousand feet — fifteen thousand — it will be cold work there, but it don't look very far on the map."

I handed him Wood on the *Sources of the Oxus*. Carnehan was deep in the *Encyclopædia*.

"They're a mixed lot," said Dravot, reflectively; "and it won't help us to know the names of their tribes. The more tribes the more they'll fight, and the better for us. From Jagdallak to Ashang. H'mm!"

"But all the information about the country is as sketchy and inaccurate as can be," I protested. "No one knows anything about it really. Here's the file of the *United Services' Institute*. Read what Bellew says."

"Blow Bellew!" said Carnehan. "Dan, they're an all-fired lot of heathens, but this book here says they think they're related to us English."

I smoked while the men pored over *Raverty, Wood*, the maps and the *Encyclopædia*.

"There is no use your waiting," said Dravot, politely. "It's about four o'clock now. We'll go before six o'clock if you want to sleep, and we won't steal any of the papers. Don't you sit up. We're two harmless lunatics, and if you come, to-morrow evening, down to the Serai we'll say good-by to you."

"You *are* two fools," I answered. "You'll be turned back at the Frontier or cut up the minute you set foot in Afghanistan. Do you want any money or a recommendation down-country? I can help you to the chance of work next week."

"Next week we shall be hard at work ourselves, thank you," said Dravot. "It isn't so easy being a King as it looks. When we've got our Kingdom in going order we'll let you know, and you can come up and help us to govern it."

"Would two lunatics make a Contrack like that!" said Carnehan, with subdued pride, showing me a greasy half-sheet of note-paper on which was written the following. I copied it, then and there, as a curiosity:—

This Contract between me and you persuing witnesseth in the name of God — Amen and so forth.

(One) That me and you will settle this matter together: i.e., to be Kings of Kafiristan.

(Two) That you and me will not while this matter is being settled, look at any Liquor, nor any Woman black, white or brown, so as to get mixed up with one or the other harmful.

(Three) That we conduct ourselves with Dignity and Discretion, and if one of us gets into trouble the other will stay by him.

Signed by you and me this day.
    Peachey Taliaferro Carnehan.
    Daniel Dravot.
    Both Gentlemen at Large.

"There was no need for the last article," said Carnehan, blushing modestly; "but it looks regular. Now you know the sort of men that loafers are — we *are* loafers, Dan, until we get out of India — and *do* you think that we could sign a Contrack like that unless we was in earnest? We have kept away from the two things that make life worth having."

"You won't enjoy your lives much longer if you are going to try this idiotic adventure. Don't set the office on fire," I said, "and go away before nine o'clock."

I left them still poring over the maps and making notes on the back of the "Contrack." "Be sure to come down to the Serai to-morrow," were their parting words.

The Kumharsen Serai is the great four-square sink of humanity where the strings of camels and horses from the North load and unload. All the nationalities of Central Asia may be found there, and most of the folk of India proper. Balkh and Bokhara there meet Bengal and Bombay, and try to draw eye-teeth. You can buy ponies, turquoises, Persian pussy-cats, saddle-bags, fat-tailed sheep and musk in the Kumharsen Serai, and get many strange things for nothing. In the afternoon I went down there to see whether my friends intended to keep their word or were lying about drunk.

A priest attired in fragments of ribbons and rags stalked up to me, gravely twisting a child's paper whirligig. Behind him was his servant, bending under the load of a crate of mud toys. The two were loading up two camels, and the inhabitants of the Serai watched them with shrieks of laughter.

"The priest is mad," said a horse-dealer to me. "He is going up to Kabul to sell toys to the Amir. He will either be raised to honor or have his head cut off. He came in here this morning and has been behaving madly ever since."

"The witless are under the protection of God," stammered a flat-cheeked Usbeg in broken Hindi. "They foretell future events."

"Would they could have foretold that my caravan would have been cut up by the Shinwaris almost within shadow of the Pass!" grunted the Eusufzai agent of a Rajputana trading-house whose goods had been feloniously diverted into the hands of other robbers just across the Border, and whose misfortunes were the laughing-stock of the bazar. "Ohé, priest, whence come you and whither do you go?"

"From Roum have I come," shouted the priest, waving his whirligig; "from Roum, blown by the breath of a hundred devils across

105

the sea! O thieves, robbers, liars, the blessing of Pir Khan on pigs, dogs, and perjurers! Who will take the Protected of God to the North to sell charms that are never still to the Amir? The camels shall not gall, the sons shall not fall sick, and the wives shall remain faithful while they are away, of the men who give me place in their caravan. Who will assist me to slipper the King of the Roos with a golden slipper with a silver heel? The protection of Pir Kahn be upon his labors!" He spread out the skirts of his gaberdine and pirouetted between the lines of tethered horses.

"There starts a caravan from Peshawar to Kabul in twenty days, *Huzrut*," said the Eusufzai trader. "My camels go therewith. Do thou also go and bring us good luck."

"I will go even now!" shouted the priest. "I will depart upon my winged camels, and be at Peshawar in a day! Ho! Hazar Mir Khan," he yelled to his servant "drive out the camels, but let me first mount my own."

He leaped on the back of his beast as it knelt, and turning round to me, cried:—"Come thou also, Sahib, a little along the road, and I will sell thee a charm — an amulet that shall make thee King of Kafiristan."

Then the light broke upon me, and I followed the two camels out of the Serai till we reached open road and the priest halted.

"What d' you think o' that?" said he in English. "Carnehan can't talk their patter, so I've made him my servant. He makes a handsome servant. 'Tisn't for nothing that I've been knocking about the country for fourteen years. Didn't I do that talk neat? We'll hitch on to a caravan at Peshawar till we get to Jagdallak, and then we'll see if we can get donkeys for our camels, and strike into Kafiristan. Whirligigs for the Amir, O Lor! Put your hand under the camel-bags and tell me what you feel."

I felt the butt of a Martini, and another and another.

"Twenty of 'em," said Dravot, placidly.

"Twenty of 'em, and ammunition to correspond, under the whirligigs and the mud dolls."

"Heaven help you if you are caught with those things!" I said. "A Martini is worth her weight in silver among the Pathans."

"Fifteen hundred rupees of capital — every rupee we could beg, borrow, or steal — are invested on these two camels," said Dravot. "We won't get caught. We're going through the Khaiber with a regular caravan. Who'd touch a poor mad priest?"

"Have you got everything you want?" I asked, overcome with astonishment.

"Not yet, but we shall soon. Give us a momento of your kindness, *Brother*. You did me a service yesterday, and that time in Marwar. Half my Kingdom shall you have, as the saying is." I slipped a small charm compass from my watch-chain and handed it up to the priest.

"Good-by," said Dravot, giving me his hand cautiously. "It's the last time we'll shake hands with an Englishman these many days. Shake hands with him, Carnehan," he cried, as the second camel passed me.

Carnehan leaned down and shook hands. Then the camels passed away along the dusty road, and I was left alone to wonder. My eye could detect no failure in the disguises. The scene in the Serai attested that they were complete to the native mind. There was just the chance, therefore, that Carnehan and Dravot would be able to wander through Afghanistan without detection. But, beyond, they would find death, certain and awful death.

Ten days later a native friend of mine, giving me the news of the day from Peshawar, wound up his letter with:— "There has been much laughter here on account of a certain mad priest who is going in his estimation to sell petty gauds and insignificant trinkets which he ascribes as great charms to H. H. the Amir of Bokhara. He passed through Peshawar and associated himself to the Second Summer caravan that goes to Kabul. The merchants are pleased because through superstition they imagine that such mad fellows bring good-fortune."

The two then, were beyond the Border. I would have prayed for them, but, that night, a real King died in Europe, and demanded an obituary notice.

* * * * *

The wheel of the world swings through the same phases again and again. Summer passed and winter thereafter, and came and passed again. The daily paper continued and I with it, and upon the third summer there fell a hot night, a night-issue, and a strained waiting for something to be telegraphed from the other side of the world, exactly as had happened before. A few great men had died in the past two years, the machines worked with more clatter, and some of the trees in the Office garden were a few feet taller. But that was all the difference.

I passed over to the press-room, and went through just such a scene as I have already described. The nervous tension was stronger than it had been two years before, and I felt the heat more acutely. At three o'clock I cried, "Print off," and turned to go, when there crept to my chair what was left of a man. He was bent into a circle, his head was sunk between his shoulders, and he moved his feet one over the other like a bear. I could hardly see whether he walked or crawled — this rag-wrapped, whining cripple who addressed me by name, crying that he was come back. "Can you give me a drink?" he whimpered. "For the Lord's sake, give me a drink!"

I went back to the office, the man following with groans of pain, and I turned up the lamp.

"Don't you know me?" he gasped, dropping into a chair, and he turned his drawn face, surmounted by a shock of gray hair, to the light.

I looked at him intently. Once before had I seen eyebrows that met over the nose in an inch-broad black band, but for the life of me I could not tell where.

"I don't know you," I said, handing him the whiskey. "What can I do for you?"

He took a gulp of the spirit raw, and shivered in spite of the suffocating heat.

"I've come back," he repeated; "and I was the King of Kafiristan — me and Dravot — crowned Kings we was! In this office we settled it — you setting there and giving us the books. I am Peachey — Peachey Taliaferro Carnehan, and you've been setting here ever since — O Lord!"

I was more than a little astonished, and expressed my feelings accordingly.

"It's true," said Carnehan, with a dry cackle, nursing his feet which were wrapped in rags. "True as gospel. Kings we were, with crowns upon our heads — me and Dravot — poor Dan — oh, poor, poor Dan, that would never take advice, not though I begged of him!"

"Take the whiskey," I said, "and take your own time. Tell me all you can recollect of everything from beginning to end. You got across the border on your camels, Dravot dressed as a mad priest and you his servant. Do you remember that?"

"I ain't mad — yet, but I will be that way soon. Of course I remember. Keep looking at me, or maybe my words will go all to pieces. Keep looking at me in my eyes and don't say anything."

I leaned forward and looked into his face as steadily as I could. He dropped one hand upon the table and I grasped it by the wrist. It was twisted like a bird's claw, and upon the back was a ragged, red, diamond-shaped scar.

"No, don't look there. Look at *me*," said Carnehan.

"That comes afterwards, but for the Lord's sake don't distrack me. We left with that caravan, me and Dravot, playing all sorts of antics to amuse the people we were with. Dravot used to make us laugh in the evenings when all the people was cooking their dinners — cooking their dinners, and … what did they do then? They lit little fires with sparks that went into Dravot's beard, and we all laughed — fit to die. Little red fires they was, going into Dravot's big red beard — so funny." His eyes left mine and he smiled foolishly.

"You went as far as Jagdallak with that caravan," I said at a venture, "after you had lit those fires. To Jagdallak, where you turned off to try to get into Kafiristan."

"No, we didn't neither. What are you talking about? We turned off before Jagdallak, because we heard the roads was good. But they wasn't good enough for our two camels — mine and Dravot's. When we left the caravan, Dravot took off all his clothes and mine too, and said we would be heathen, because the Kafirs didn't allow Mohammedans to talk to them. So we dressed betwixt and between, and such a sight as Daniel Dravot I never saw yet nor expect to see again. He burned half his beard, and slung a sheep-skin over his shoulder, and shaved his head into patterns. He shaved mine, too, and made me wear outrageous things to look like a heathen. That was in a most mountaineous country, and our camels couldn't go along any more because of the mountains. They were tall and black, and coming home I saw them fight like wild goats — there are lots of goats in Kafiristan. And these mountains, they never keep still, no more than the goats. Always fighting they are, and don't let you sleep at night."

"Take some more whiskey," I said, very slowly. "What did you and Daniel Dravot do when the camels could go no further because of the rough roads that led into Kafiristan?"

"What did which do? There was a party called Peachey Taliaferro Carnehan that was with Dravot. Shall I tell you about him? He died out there in the cold. Slap from the bridge fell old Peachey, turning and twisting in the air like a penny whirligig that you can sell to the Amir — No; they was two for three ha'pence, those whirligigs, or I am much mistaken and woful sore. And then these camels were no use, and Peachey said to Dravot — 'For the Lord's sake, let's get out of this before our

110

heads are chopped off,' and with that they killed the camels all among the mountains, not having anything in particular to eat, but first they took off the boxes with the guns and the ammunition, till two men came along driving four mules. Dravot up and dances in front of them, singing, — 'Sell me four mules.' Says the first man, — 'If you are rich enough to buy, you are rich enough to rob;' but before ever he could put his hand to his knife, Dravot breaks his neck over his knee, and the other party runs away. So Carnehan loaded the mules with the rifles that was taken off the camels, and together we starts forward into those bitter cold mountainous parts, and never a road broader than the back of your hand."

He paused for a moment, while I asked him if he could remember the nature of the country through which he had journeyed.

"I am telling you as straight as I can, but my head isn't as good as it might be. They drove nails through it to make me hear better how Dravot died. The country was mountainous and the mules were most contrary, and the inhabitants was dispersed and solitary. They went up and up, and down and down, and that other party Carnehan, was imploring of Dravot not to sing and whistle so loud, for fear of bringing down the tremenjus avalanches. But Dravot says that if a King couldn't sing it wasn't worth being King, and whacked the mules over the rump, and never took no heed for ten cold days. We came to a big level valley all among the mountains, and the mules were near dead, so we killed them, not having anything in special for them or us to eat. We sat upon the boxes, and played odd and even with the cartridges that was jolted out.

"Then ten men with bows and arrows ran down that valley, chasing twenty men with bows and arrows, and the row was tremenjus. They was fair men — fairer than you or me — with yellow hair and remarkable well built. Says Dravot, unpacking the guns — 'This is the beginning of the business. We'll fight for the ten men,' and with that he fires two rifles at the twenty men and drops one of them at two hundred yards from the rock where we was sitting. The other men began to run, but Carnehan and Dravot sits on the boxes picking them off at all ranges, up and down the valley. Then we goes up to the ten men that had run across the snow too, and they fires a footy little arrow at us. Dravot he shoots above their heads and they all falls down flat. Then he walks over them and kicks them, and then he lifts them up and shakes hands all around to make them friendly like. He calls them and gives them the boxes to carry, and waves his hand for all the world as though he was King already. They takes the boxes and him across the valley and up the hill into a pine wood on the top, where there was half a dozen big stone idols. Dravot he goes to the biggest — a fellow they call Imbra — and lays a rifle and a cartridge at his feet, rubbing his nose respectful with his own nose, patting him on the head, and saluting in front of it. He turns round to the men and nods his head, and says, — 'That's all right. I'm in the know too, and these old jim-jams are my friends.' Then he opens his mouth and points down it, and when the first man brings him food, he says — 'No;' and when the second man brings him food, he says — 'No;' but when one of the old priests and the boss of the village brings him food, he says — 'Yes;' very haughty, and eats it slow. That was how we came to our first village, without any trouble, just as though we had tumbled from the skies. But we tumbled from one of those damned rope-bridges, you see, and you couldn't expect a man to laugh much after that."

"Take some more whiskey and go on," I said. "That was the first village you came into. How did you get to be King?"

"I wasn't King," said Carnehan. "Dravot he was the King, and a handsome man he looked with the gold crown on his head and all. Him and the other party stayed in that village, and every morning Dravot sat by the side of old Imbra, and the people came and worshipped. That was Dravot's order. Then a lot of men came into the valley, and Carnehan and Dravot picks them off with the rifles before they knew where they was, and runs down into the valley and up again the other side, and finds another village, same as the first one, and the people all falls down flat on their faces, and Dravot says, — 'Now what is the trouble between you two villages?' and the people points to a woman, as fair as you or me, that was carried off, and Dravot takes her back to the first village and counts up the dead — eight there was. For each dead man Dravot pours a little milk on the ground and waves his arms like a whirligig and, 'That's all right,' says he. Then he and Carnehan takes the big boss of each village by the arm and walks them down into the valley, and shows them how to scratch a line with a spear right down the valley, and gives each a sod of turf from both sides o' the line. Then all the people comes down and shouts like the devil and all, and Dravot says, — 'Go and dig the land, and be fruitful and multiply,' which they did, though they didn't understand. Then we asks the names of things in their lingo — bread and water and fire and idols and such, and Dravot leads the priest of each village up to the idol, and says he must sit there and judge the people, and if anything goes wrong he is to be shot.

"Next week they was all turning up the land in the valley as quiet as bees and much prettier, and the priests heard all the complaints and told Dravot in dumb show what it was about. 'That's just the beginning,' says Dravot. 'They think we're gods.' He and Carnehan picks out twenty good men and shows them how to click off a rifle, and form fours, and advance in line, and they was very pleased to do so, and clever to see the hang of it. Then he takes out his pipe and his baccy-pouch and leaves one at one village, and one at the other, and off we two goes to see what was to be done in the next valley. That was all rock, and there was a little village there, and Carnehan says, — 'Send 'em to the old valley to plant,' and takes 'em there and gives 'em some land that wasn't took before. They were a poor lot, and we blooded 'em with a kid before letting 'em into the new Kingdom. That was to impress the people, and then they settled down quiet, and Carnehan went back to Dravot who had got into another valley, all snow and ice and most mountainous. There was no people there and the Army got afraid, so Dravot shoots one of them, and goes on till he finds some people in a village, and the Army explains that unless the people wants to be killed they had better not shoot their little matchlocks; for they had matchlocks. We makes friends with the priest and I stays there alone with two of the Army, teaching the men how to drill, and a thundering big Chief comes across the snow with kettledrums and horns twanging, because he heard there was a new god kicking about. Carnehan sights for the brown of the men half a mile across the snow and wings one of them. Then he sends a message to the Chief that, unless he wished to be killed, he must come and shake hands with me and leave his arms behind. The Chief comes alone first, and Carnehan shakes hands with him and whirls his arms about, same as Dravot used, and very much surprised that Chief was, and strokes my eyebrows. Then Carnehan goes alone to the Chief, and asks him in dumb show if he had an enemy he hated. 'I have,' says the Chief. So Carnehan weeds out the pick of his men, and sets the two of the Army to show them drill and at the end of two weeks the men can manœuvre about as well as Volunteers. So he marches with the Chief to a great big plain on the top of a mountain, and the Chiefs men rushes into a village and takes it; we three Martinis firing into the brown of the enemy. So we took that village too, and I gives the Chief a rag from my coat and says, 'Occupy till I come': which was scriptural. By way of a reminder, when me and the Army was eighteen hundred yards away, I drops a bullet near him standing on the snow, and all the people falls flat on their faces. Then I sends a letter to Dravot, wherever he be by land or by sea."

At the risk of throwing the creature out of train I interrupted, — "How could you write a letter up yonder?"

"The letter? — Oh! — The letter! Keep looking at me between the eyes, please. It was a string-talk letter, that we'd learned the way of it from a blind beggar in the Punjab."

I remember that there had once come to the office a blind man with a knotted twig and a piece of string which he wound round the twig according to some cypher of his own. He could, after the lapse of days or hours, repeat the sentence which he had reeled up. He had reduced the alphabet to eleven primitive sounds; and tried to teach me his method, but failed.

"I sent that letter to Dravot," said Carnehan; "and told him to come back because this Kingdom was growing too big for me to handle, and then I struck for the first valley, to see how the priests were working. They called the village we took along with the Chief, Bashkai, and the first village we took, Er-Heb. The priest at Er-Heb was doing all right, but they had a lot of pending cases about land to show me, and some men from

114

another village had been firing arrows at night. I went out and looked for that village and fired four rounds at it from a thousand yards. That used all the cartridges I cared to spend, and I waited for Dravot, who had been away two or three months, and I kept my people quiet.

"One morning I heard the devil's own noise of drums and horns, and Dan Dravot marches down the hill with his Army and a tail of hundreds of men, and, which was the most amazing — a great gold crown on his head. 'My Gord, Carnehan,' says Daniel, 'this is a tremenjus business, and we've got the whole country as far as it's worth having. I am the son of Alexander by Queen Semiramis, and you're my younger brother and a god too! It's the biggest thing we've ever seen. I've been marching and fighting for six weeks with the Army, and every footy little village for fifty miles has come in rejoiceful; and more than that, I've got the key of the whole show, as you'll see, and I've got a crown for you! I told 'em to make two of 'em at a place called Shu, where the gold lies in the rock like suet in mutton. Gold I've seen, and turquoise I've kicked out of the cliffs, and there's garnets in the sands of the river, and here's a chunk of amber that a man brought me. Call up all the priests and, here, take your crown.'

"One of the men opens a black hair bag and I slips the crown on. It was too small and too heavy, but I wore it for the glory. Hammered gold it was — five pound weight, like a hoop of a barrel.

"'Peachey,' says Dravot, 'we don't want to fight no more. The Craft's the trick so help me!' and he brings forward that same Chief that I left at Bashkai — Billy Fish we called him afterwards, because he was so like Billy Fish that drove the big tank-engine at Mach on the Bolan in the old days. 'Shake hands with him,' says Dravot, and I shook hands and nearly dropped, for Billy Fish gave me the Grip. I said nothing, but tried him with the Fellow Craft Grip. He answers, all right, and I tried the Master's Grip, but that was a slip. 'A Fellow Craft he is!' I says to Dan. 'Does he know the word?' 'He does,' says Dan, 'and all the priests know. It's a miracle! The Chiefs and the priest can work a Fellow Craft Lodge in a way that's very like ours, and they've cut the marks on the rocks, but they don't know the Third Degree, and they've come to find out. It's Gord's Truth. I've known these long years that the Afghans knew up to the Fellow Craft Degree, but this is a miracle. A god and a Grand-Master of the Craft am I, and a Lodge in the Third Degree I will open, and we'll raise the head priests and the Chiefs of the villages.'

"'It's against all the law,' I says, 'holding a Lodge without warrant from any one; and we never held office in any Lodge.'

"'It's a master-stroke of policy,' says Dravot. 'It means running the country as easy as a four-wheeled bogy on a down grade. We can't stop to inquire now, or they'll turn against us. I've forty Chiefs at my heel, and passed and raised according to their merit they shall be. Billet these men on the villages and see that we run up a Lodge of some kind. The temple of Imbra will do for the Lodge-room. The women must make aprons as you show them. I'll hold a levee of Chiefs tonight and Lodge to-morrow.'

"I was fair rim off my legs, but I wasn't such a fool as not to see what a pull this Craft business gave us. I showed the priests' families how to make aprons of the degrees, but for Dravot's apron the blue border and marks was made of turquoise lumps on white hide, not cloth. We took a great square stone in the temple for the Master's chair, and little stones for the officers' chairs, and painted the black pavement with white squares, and did what we could to make things regular.

"At the levee which was held that night on the hillside with big bonfires, Dravot gives out that him and me were gods and sons of Alexander, and Past Grand-Masters in the Craft, and was come to make Kafiristan a country where every man should eat in peace and drink in quiet, and specially obey us. Then the Chiefs come round to shake hands, and they was so hairy and white and fair it was just shaking hands with old friends. We gave them names according as they was like men we had known in India — Billy Fish, Holly Dilworth, Pikky Kergan that was Bazar-master when I was at Mhow, and so on, and so on.

116

"*The* most amazing miracle was at Lodge next night. One of the old priests was watching us continuous, and I felt uneasy, for I knew we'd have to fudge the Ritual, and I didn't know what the men knew. The old priest was a stranger come in from beyond the village of Bashkai. The minute Dravot puts on the Master's apron that the girls had made for him, the priest fetches a whoop and a howl, and tries to overturn the stone that Dravot was sitting on. 'It's all up now,' I says. 'That comes of meddling with the Craft without warrant!' Dravot never winked an eye, not when ten priests took and tilted over the Grand-Master's chair — which was to say the stone of Imbra. The priest begins rubbing the bottom end of it to clear away the black dirt, and presently he shows all the other priests the Master's Mark, same as was on Dravot's apron, cut into the stone. Not even the priests of the temple of Imbra knew it was there. The old chap falls flat on his face at Dravot's feet and kisses 'em. 'Luck again,' says Dravot, across the Lodge to me, 'they say it's the missing Mark that no one could understand the why of. We're more than safe now.' Then he bangs the butt of his gun for a gavel and says:— 'By virtue of the authority vested in me by my own right hand and the help of Peachey, I declare myself Grand-Master of all Freemasonry in Kafiristan in this the Mother Lodge o' the country, and King of Kafiristan equally with Peachey!' At that he puts on his crown and I puts on mine — I was doing Senior Warden — and we opens the Lodge in most ample form. It was a amazing miracle! The priests moved in Lodge through the first two degrees almost without telling, as if the memory was coming back to them. After that, Peachey and Dravot raised such as was worthy — high priests and Chiefs of far-off villages. Billy Fish was the first, and I can tell you we scared the soul out of him. It was not in any way according to Ritual, but it served our turn. We didn't raise more than ten of the biggest men because we didn't want to make the Degree common. And they was clamoring to be raised.

"'In another six months,' says Dravot, 'we'll hold another Communication and see how you are working.' Then he asks them about their villages, and learns that they was fighting one against the other and were fair sick and tired of it. And when they wasn't doing that they was fighting with the Mohammedans. 'You can fight those when they come into our country,' says Dravot. 'Tell off every tenth man of your tribes for a Frontier guard, and send two hundred at a time to this valley to be drilled. Nobody is going to be shot or speared any more so long as he does well, and I know that you won't cheat me because you're white people — sons of Alexander — and not like common, black Mohammedans. You are *my* people and by God,' says he, running off into English at the end — 'I'll make a damned fine Nation of you, or I'll die in the making!'

"I can't tell all we did for the next six months because Dravot did a lot I couldn't see the hang of, and he learned their lingo in a way I never could. My work was to help the people plough, and now and again to go out with some of the Army and see what the other villages were doing, and make 'em throw rope-bridges across the ravines which cut up the country horrid. Dravot was very kind to me, but when he walked up and down in the pine wood pulling that bloody red beard of his with both fists I knew he was thinking plans I could not advise him about, and I just waited for orders.

"But Dravot never showed me disrespect before the people. They were afraid of me and the Army, but they loved Dan. He was the best of friends with the priests and the Chiefs; but any one could come across the hills with a complaint and Dravot would hear him out fair, and call four priests together and say what was to be done. He used to call in Billy Fish from Bashkai, and Pikky Kergan from Shu, and an old Chief we called Kafuzelum — it was like enough to his real name — and hold councils with 'em when there was any fighting to be done in small villages. That was his Council of War, and the four priests of Bashkai, Shu, Khawak, and Madora was his Privy Council. Between the lot of 'em they sent me, with forty men and twenty rifles, and sixty men carrying turquoises, into the Ghorband country to buy those hand-made Martini rifles, that come out of the Amir's workshops at Kabul, from one of the Amir's Herati regiments that would have sold the very teeth out of their mouths for turquoises.

"I stayed in Ghorband a month, and gave the Governor the pick of my baskets for hush-money, and bribed the colonel of the regiment some more, and, between the two and the tribes-people, we got more than a hundred hand-made Martinis, a hundred good Kohat Jezails that'll throw to six hundred yards, and forty manloads of very bad ammunition for the rifles. I came back with what I had, and distributed 'em among the men that the Chiefs sent in to me to drill. Dravot was too busy to attend to those things, but the old Army that we first made helped me, and we turned out five hundred men that could drill, and two hundred that knew how to hold arms pretty straight. Even those cork-screwed, hand-made guns was a miracle to them. Dravot talked big about powder-shops and factories, walking up and down in the pine wood when the winter was coming on.

"'I won't make a Nation,' says he. 'I'll make an Empire! These men aren't niggers; they're English! Look at their eyes — look at their mouths. Look at the way they stand up. They sit on chairs in their own houses. They're the Lost Tribes, or something like it, and they've grown to be English. I'll take a census in the spring if the priests don't get frightened. There must be a fair two million of 'em in these hills. The villages are full o' little children. Two million people — two hundred and fifty thousand fighting men — and all English! They only want the rifles and a little drilling. Two hundred and fifty thousand men, ready to cut in on Russia's right flank when she tries for India! Peachey, man,' he says, chewing his beard in great hunks, 'we shall be Emperors — Emperors of the Earth! Rajah Brooke will be a suckling to us. I'll treat with the Viceroy on equal terms. I'll ask him to send me twelve picked English — twelve that I know of — to help us govern a bit. There's Mackray, Sergeant-pensioner at Segowli — many's the good dinner he's given me, and his wife a pair of trousers. There's Donkin, the Warder of Tounghoo Jail; there's hundreds that I could lay my hand on if I was in India. The Viceroy shall do it for me. I'll send a man through in the spring for those men, and I'll write for a dispensation from the Grand Lodge for what I've done as Grand-Master. That — and all the Sniders that'll be thrown out when the native troops in India take up the Martini. They'll be worn smooth, but they'll do for fighting in these hills. Twelve English, a hundred thousand Sniders run through the Amir's country in driblets — I'd be content with twenty thousand in one year — and we'd be an Empire. When everything was ship-shape, I'd hand over the crown — this crown I'm wearing now — to Queen Victoria on my knees, and she'd say:— "Rise up, Sir Daniel Dravot." Oh, its big! It's big, I tell you! But there's so much to be done in every place — Bashkai, Khawak, Shu, and everywhere else.'

"'What is it?' I says. 'There are no more men coming in to be drilled this autumn. Look at those fat, black clouds. They're bringing the snow.'

"'It isn't that,' says Daniel, putting his hand very hard on my shoulder; 'and I don't wish to say anything that's against you, for no other living man would have followed me and made me what I am as you have done. You're a first-class Commander-in-Chief, and the people know you; but — it's a big country, and somehow you can't help me, Peachey, in the way I want to be helped.'

"'Go to your blasted priests, then!' I said, and I was sorry when I made that remark, but it did hurt me sore to find Daniel talking so superior when I'd drilled all the men, and done all he told me.

"'Don't let's quarrel, Peachey,' says Daniel without cursing. 'You're a King too, and the half of this Kingdom is yours; but can't you see, Peachey, we want cleverer men than us now — three or four of 'em that we can scatter about for our Deputies? It's a hugeous great State, and I can't always tell the right thing to do, and I haven't time for all I want to do, and here's the winter coming on and all.' He put half his beard into his mouth, and it was as red as the gold of his crown.

"'I'm sorry, Daniel,' says I. 'I've done all I could. I've drilled the men and shown the people how to stack their oats better, and I've brought in those tinware rifles from Ghorband — but I know what you're driving at. I take it Kings always feel oppressed that way.'

"'There's another thing too,' says Dravot, walking up and down. 'The winter's coming and these people won't be giving much trouble, and if they do we can't move about. I want a wife.'

"'For Gord's sake leave the women alone!' I says. 'We've both got all the work we can, though I *am* a fool. Remember the Contrack, and keep clear o' women.'

"'The Contrack only lasted till such time as we was Kings; and Kings we have been these months past,' says Dravot, weighing his crown in his hand. 'You go get a wife too, Peachey — a nice, strappin', plump girl that'll keep you warm in the winter. They're prettier than English girls, and we can take the pick of 'em. Boil 'em once or twice in hot water, and they'll come as fair as chicken and ham.'

"'Don't tempt me!' I says. 'I will not have any dealings with a woman not till we are a dam' side more settled than we are now. I've been doing the work o' two men, and you've been doing the work o' three. Let's lie off a bit, and see if we can get some better tobacco from Afghan country and run in some good liquor; but no women.'

"'Who's talking o' *women*?' says Dravot. 'I said *wife* — a Queen to breed a King's son for the King. A Queen out of the strongest tribe, that'll make them your blood-brothers, and that'll lie by your side and tell you all the people thinks about you and their own affairs. That's what I want.'

"'Do you remember that Bengali woman I kept at Mogul Serai when I was plate-layer?' says I. 'A fat lot o' good she was to me. She taught me the lingo and one or two other things; but what happened? She ran away with the Station Master's servant and half my month's pay. Then she turned up at Dadur Junction in tow of a half-caste, and had the impidence to say I was her husband — all among the drivers of the running-shed!'

"'We've done with that,' says Dravot. 'These women are whiter than you or me, and a Queen I will have for the winter months.'

"'For the last time o' asking, Dan, do *not*,' I says. 'It'll only bring us harm. The Bible says that Kings ain't to waste their strength on women, 'specially when they've got a new raw Kingdom to work over.'

"'For the last time of answering, I will,' said Dravot, and he went away through the pine-trees looking like a big red devil. The low sun hit his crown and beard on one side, and the two blazed like hot coals.

"But getting a wife was not as easy as Dan thought. He put it before the Council, and there was no answer till Billy Fish said that he'd better ask the girls. Dravot damned them all round. 'What's wrong with me?' he shouts, standing by the idol Imbra. 'Am I a dog or am I not enough of a man for your wenches? Haven't I put the shadow of my hand over this country? Who stopped the last Afghan raid?' It was me really, but Dravot was too angry to remember. 'Who bought your guns? Who repaired the bridges? Who's the Grand-Master of the sign cut in the stone?' and he thumped his hand on the block that he used to sit on in Lodge, and at Council, which opened like Lodge always. Billy Fish said nothing and no more did the others. 'Keep your hair on, Dan,' said I; 'and ask the girls. That's how it's done at home, and these people are quite English.'

"'The marriage of a King is a matter of State,' says Dan, in a white-hot rage, for he could feel, I hope, that he was going against his better mind. He walked out of the Council-room, and the others sat still, looking at the ground.

"'Billy Fish,' says I to the Chief of Bashkai, 'what's the difficulty here? A straight answer to a true friend.' 'You know,' says Billy Fish. 'How should a man tell you who know everything? How can daughters of men marry gods or devils? It's not proper.'

"I remembered something like that in the Bible; but if, after seeing us as long as they had, they still believed we were gods it wasn't for me to undeceive them.

"'A god can do anything,' says I. 'If the King is fond of a girl he'll not let her die.' 'She'll have to,' said Billy Fish. 'There are all sorts of gods and devils in these mountains, and now and again a girl marries one of them and isn't seen any more. Besides, you two know the Mark cut in the stone. Only the gods know that. We thought you were men till you showed the sign of the Master.'

"'I wished then that we had explained about the loss of the genuine secrets of a Master-Mason at the first go-off; but I said nothing. All that night there was a blowing of horns in a little dark temple half-way down the hill, and I heard a girl crying fit to die. One of the priests told us that she was being prepared to marry the King.

"'I'll have no nonsense of that kind,' says Dan. 'I don't want to interfere with your customs, but I'll take my own wife.' 'The girl's a little bit afraid,' says the priest. 'She thinks she's going to die, and they are a-heartening of her up down in the temple.'

"'Hearten her very tender, then,' says Dravot, 'or I'll hearten you with the butt of a gun so that you'll never want to be heartened again.' He licked his lips, did Dan, and stayed up walking about more than half the night, thinking of the wife that he was going to get in the morning. I wasn't any means comfortable, for I knew that dealings with a woman in foreign parts, though you was a crowned King twenty times over, could not but be risky. I got up very early in the morning while Dravot was asleep, and I saw the priests talking together in whispers, and the Chiefs talking together too, and they looked at me out of the corners of their eyes.

"'What is up, Fish?' I says to the Bashkai man, who was wrapped up in his furs and looking splendid to behold.

"'I can't rightly say,' says he; 'but if you can induce the King to drop all this nonsense about marriage, you'll be doing him and me and yourself a great service.'

"'That I do believe,' says I. 'But sure, you know, Billy, as well as me, having fought against and for us, that the King and me are nothing more than two of the finest men that God Almighty ever made. Nothing more, I do assure you.'

"'That may be,' says Billy Fish, 'and yet I should be sorry if it was.' He sinks his head upon his great fur cloak for a minute and thinks. 'King,' says he, 'be you man or god or devil, I'll stick by you to-day. I have twenty of my men with me, and they will follow me. We'll go to Bashkai until the storm blows over.'

"A little snow had fallen in the night, and everything was white except the greasy fat clouds that blew down and down from the north. Dravot came out with his crown on his head, swinging his arms and stamping his feet, and looking more pleased than Punch.

"'For the last time, drop it, Dan,' says I in a whisper. 'Billy Fish here says that there will be a row.'

"'A row among my people!' says Dravot. 'Not much. Peachy, you're a fool not to get a wife too. Where's the girl?' says he with a voice as loud as the braying of a jackass. 'Call up all the Chiefs and priests, and let the Emperor see if his wife suits him.'

"There was no need to call any one. They were all there leaning on their guns and spears round the clearing in the centre of the pine wood. A deputation of priests went down to the little temple to bring up the girl, and the horns blew up fit to wake the dead. Billy Fish saunters round and gets as close to Daniel as he could, and behind him stood his twenty men with matchlocks. Not a man of them under six feet. I was next to Dravot, and behind me was twenty men of the regular Army. Up comes the girl, and a strapping wench she was, covered with silver and turquoises but white as death, and looking back every minute at the priests.

"'She'll do,' said Dan, looking her over. 'What's to be afraid of, lass? Come and kiss me.' He puts his arm round her. She shuts her eyes, gives a bit of a squeak, and down goes her face in the side of Dan's flaming red beard.

"'The slut's bitten me!' says he, clapping his hand to his neck, and, sure enough, his hand was red with blood. Billy Fish and two of his matchlock-men catches hold of Dan by the shoulders and drags him into the Bashkai lot, while the priests howls in their lingo, — 'Neither god nor devil but a man!' I was all taken aback, for a priest cut at me in front, and the Army behind began firing into the Bashkai men.

"'God A-mighty!' says Dan. 'What is the meaning o' this?'

"'Come back! Come away!' says Billy Fish. 'Ruin and Mutiny is the matter. We'll break for Bashkai if we can.'

"I tried to give some sort of orders to my men — the men o' the regular Army — but it was no use, so I fired into the brown of 'em with an English Martini and drilled three beggars in a line. The valley was full of shouting, howling creatures, and every soul was shrieking, 'Not a god nor a devil but only a man!' The Bashkai troops stuck to Billy Fish all they were worth, but their matchlocks wasn't half as good as the Kabul breech-loaders, and four of them dropped. Dan was bellowing like a bull, for he was very wrathy; and Billy Fish had a hard job to prevent him running out at the crowd.

"'We can't stand,' says Billy Fish. 'Make a run for it down the valley! The whole place is against us.' The matchlock-men ran, and we went down the valley in spite of Dravot's protestations. He was swearing horribly and crying out that he was a King. The priests rolled great stones on us, and the regular Army fired hard, and there wasn't more than six men, not counting Dan, Billy Fish, and Me, that came down to the bottom of the valley alive.

"'Then they stopped firing and the horns in the temple blew again. 'Come away — for Gord's sake come away!' says Billy Fish. 'They'll send runners out to all the villages before ever we get to Bashkai. I can protect you there, but I can't do anything now.'

"My own notion is that Dan began to go mad in his head from that hour. He stared up and down like a stuck pig. Then he was all for walking back alone and killing the priests with his bare hands; which he could have done. 'An Emperor am I,' says Daniel, 'and next year I shall be a Knight of the Queen.

"'All right, Dan,' says I; 'but come along now while there's time.'

"'It's your fault,' says he, 'for not looking after your Army better. There was mutiny in the midst, and you didn't know — you damned engine-driving, plate-laying, missionary's-pass-hunting hound!' He sat upon a rock and called me every foul name he could lay tongue to. I was too heart-sick to care, though it was all his foolishness that brought the smash.

"'I'm sorry, Dan,' says I, 'but there's no accounting for natives. This business is our Fifty-Seven. Maybe we'll make something out of it yet, when we've got to Bashkai.'

"'Let's get to Bashkai, then,' says Dan, 'and, by God, when I come back here again I'll sweep the valley so there isn't a bug in a blanket left!'

"'We walked all that day, and all that night Dan was stumping up and down on the snow, chewing his beard and muttering to himself.

"'There's no hope o' getting clear,' said Billy Fish. 'The priests will have sent runners to the villages to say that you are only men. Why didn't you stick on as gods till things was more settled? I'm a dead man,' says Billy Fish, and he throws himself down on the snow and begins to pray to his gods.

"Next morning we was in a cruel bad country — all up and down, no level ground at all, and no food either. The six Bashkai men looked at Billy Fish hungry-wise as if they wanted to ask something, but they said never a word. At noon we came to the top of a flat mountain all covered with snow, and when we climbed up into it, behold, there was an army in position waiting in the middle!

"'The runners have been very quick,' says Billy Fish, with a little bit of a laugh. 'They are waiting for us.'

126

"Three or four men began to fire from the enemy's side, and a chance shot took Daniel in the calf of the leg. That brought him to his senses. He looks across the snow at the Army, and sees the rifles that we had brought into the country.

"'We're done for,' says he. 'They are Englishmen, these people, — and it's my blasted nonsense that has brought you to this. Get back, Billy Fish, and take your men away; you've done what you could, and now cut for it. Carnehan,' says he, 'shake hands with me and go along with Billy. Maybe they won't kill you. I'll go and meet 'em alone. It's me that did it. Me, the King!'

"'Go!' says I. 'Go to Hell, Dan. I'm with you here. Billy Fish, you clear out, and we two will meet those folk.'

"'I'm a Chief,' says Billy Fish, quite quiet. 'I stay with you. My men can go.'

"The Bashkai fellows didn't wait for a second word but ran off, and Dan and Me and Billy Fish walked across to where the drums were drumming and the horns were horning. It was cold-awful cold. I've got that cold in the back of my head now. There's a lump of it there."

The punkah-coolies had gone to sleep. Two kerosene lamps were blazing in the office, and the perspiration poured down my face and splashed on the blotter as I leaned forward. Carnehan was shivering, and I feared that his mind might go. I wiped my face, took a fresh grip of the piteously mangled hands, and said:— "What happened after that?"

The momentary shift of my eyes had broken the clear current.

"What was you pleased to say?" whined Carnehan. "They took them without any sound. Not a little whisper all along the snow, not though the King knocked down the first man that set hand on him — not though old Peachey fired his last cartridge into the brown of 'em. Not a single solitary sound did those swines make. They just closed up, tight, and I tell you their furs stunk. There was a man called Billy Fish, a good friend of us all, and they cut his throat, Sir, then and there, like a pig; and

127

the King kicks up the bloody snow and says:— 'We've had a dashed fine run for our money. What's coming next?' But Peachey, Peachey Taliaferro, I tell you, Sir, in confidence as betwixt two friends, he lost his head, Sir. No, he didn't neither. The King lost his head, so he did, all along o' one of those cunning rope-bridges. Kindly let me have the paper-cutter, Sir. It tilted this way. They marched him a mile across that snow to a rope-bridge over a ravine with a river at the bottom. You may have seen such. They prodded him behind like an ox. 'Damn your eyes!' says the King. 'D'you suppose I can't die like a gentleman?' He turns to Peachey — Peachey that was crying like a child. 'I've brought you to this, Peachey,' says he. 'Brought you out of your happy life to be killed in Kafiristan, where you was late Commander-in-Chief of the Emperor's forces. Say you forgive me, Peachey.' 'I do,' says Peachey. 'Fully and freely do I forgive you, Dan.' 'Shake hands, Peachey,' says he. 'I'm going now.' Out he goes, looking neither right nor left, and when he was plumb in the middle of those dizzy dancing ropes, 'Cut, you beggars,' he shouts; and they cut, and old Dan fell, turning round and round and round, twenty thousand miles, for he took half an hour to fall till he struck the water, and I could see his body caught on a rock with the gold crown close beside.

"But do you know what they did to Peachey between two pine-trees? They crucified him, sir, as Peachey's hands will show. They used wooden pegs for his hands and his feet; and he didn't die. He hung there and screamed, and they took him down next day, and said it was a miracle that he wasn't dead. They took him down — poor old Peachey that hadn't done them any harm — that hadn't done them any…"

He rocked to and fro and wept bitterly, wiping his eyes with the back of his scarred hands and moaning like a child for some ten minutes.

"They was cruel enough to feed him up in the temple, because they said he was more of a god than old Daniel that was a man. Then they turned him out on the snow, and told him to go home, and Peachey came home in about a year, begging along the roads quite safe; for Daniel Dravot he walked before and said:— 'Come along, Peachey. It's a big thing we're doing.' The mountains they danced at night, and the mountains they tried to fall on Peachey's head, but Dan he held up his hand, and Peachey came along bent double. He never let go of Dan's hand, and he never let go of Dan's head. They gave it to him as a present in the temple, to remind him not to come again, and though the crown was pure gold, and Peachey was starving, never would Peachey sell the same. You knew Dravot, sir! You knew Right Worshipful Brother Dravot! Look at him now!"

He fumbled in the mass of rags round his bent waist; brought out a black horsehair bag embroidered with silver thread; and shook therefrom on to my table — the dried, withered head of Daniel Dravot! The morning sun that had long been paling the lamps struck the red beard and blind sunken eyes; struck, too, a heavy circlet of gold studded with raw turquoises, that Carnehan placed tenderly on the battered temples.

"You behold now," said Carnehan, "the Emperor in his habit as he lived — the King of Kafiristan with his crown upon his head. Poor old Daniel that was a monarch once!"

I shuddered, for, in spite of defacements manifold, I recognized the head of the man of Marwar Junction. Carnehan rose to go. I attempted to stop him. He was not fit to walk abroad. "Let me take away the whiskey, and give me a little money," he gasped. "I was a King once. I'll go to the Deputy Commissioner and ask to set in the Poor-house till I get my health. No, thank you, I can't wait till you get a carriage for me. I've urgent private affairs — in the south — at Marwar."

He shambled out of the office and departed in the direction of the Deputy Commissioner's house. That day at noon I had occasion to go down the blinding hot Mall, and I saw a crooked man crawling along the white dust of the roadside, his hat in his hand, quavering dolorously after the fashion of street-singers at Home. There was not a soul in sight, and he was out of all possible earshot of the houses. And he sang through his nose, turning his head from right to left:—

"The Son of Man goes forth to war,
 A golden crown to gain;

His blood-red banner streams afar—
 Who follows in his train?"

I waited to hear no more, but put the poor wretch into my carriage and drove him off to the nearest missionary for eventual transfer to the Asylum. He repeated the hymn twice while he was with me whom he did not in the least recognize, and I left him singing to the missionary.

Two days later I inquired after his welfare of the Superintendent of the Asylum.

"He was admitted suffering from sun-stroke. He died early yesterday morning," said the Superintendent. "Is it true that he was half an hour bareheaded in the sun at midday?"

"Yes," said I, "but do you happen to know if he had anything upon him by any chance when he died?"

"Not to my knowledge," said the Superintendent.

And there the matter rests.

EIGHT MASONIC POEMS

The Mother Lodge

There was Rundle, Station Master,
  An' Beazeley of the Rail,
An' 'Ackman, Commissariat,
  An' Donkin' o' the Jail;
An' Blake, Conductor-Sergeant,
  Our Master twice was 'e,
With 'im that kept the Europe-shop,
  Old Framjee Eduljee.

Outside – "Sergeant! Sir! Salute! Salaam!"
Inside – "Brother," an' it doesn't do no 'arm.
We met upon the Level an' we parted on the Square,
An' I was junior Deacon in my Mother-Lodge out there!

We'd Bola Nath, Accountant,
  An' Saul the Aden Jew,
An' Din Mohammed, draughtsman
  Of the Survey Office too;
There was Babu Chuckerbutty,
  An' Amir Singh the Sikh,
An' Castro from the fittin'-sheds,
  The Roman Catholick!

We 'adn't good regalia,
  An' our Lodge was old an' bare,
But we knew the Ancient Landmarks,
  An' we kep' 'em to a hair;
An' lookin' on it backwards
  It often strikes me thus,
There ain't such things as infidels,
  Excep', per'aps, it's us.

For monthly, after Labour,
  We'd all sit down and smoke
(We dursn't give no banquets,

Lest a Brother's caste were broke),
An' man on man got talkin'
  Religion an' the rest,
An' every man comparin'
  Of the God 'e knew the best.

So man on man got talkin',
  An' not a Brother stirred
Till mornin' waked the parrots
  An' that dam' brain-fever-bird.
We'd say 'twas 'ighly curious,
  An' we'd all ride 'ome to bed,
With Mo'ammed, God, an' Shiva
  Changin' pickets in our 'ead.

Full oft on Guv'ment service
  This rovin' foot 'ath pressed,
An' bore fraternal greetin's
  To the Lodges east an' west,
Accordin' as commanded.
  From Kohat to Singapore,
But I wish that I might see them
  In my Mother-Lodge once more!

I wish that I might see them,
  My Brethren black an' brown,
With the trichies smellin' pleasant
  An' the hog-darn passin' down;
An' the old khansamah snorin'
  On the bottle-khana floor,
Like a Master in good standing
  With my Mother-Lodge once more.

Outside – "Sergeant! Sir! Salute! Salaam!"
Inside – "Brother," an' it doesn't do no 'arm.
We met upon the Level an' we parted on the Square,
An' I was Junior Deacon in my Mother-Lodge out there!

If –

If you can keep your head when all about you
  Are losing theirs and blaming it on you,
If you can trust yourself when all men doubt you,
  But make allowance for their doubting too;
If you can wait and not be tired by waiting,
  Or being lied about, don't deal in lies,
Or being hated, don't give way to hating,
  And yet don't look too good, nor talk too wise:

If you can dream - and not make dreams your master;
  If you can think - and not make thoughts your aim;
If you can meet with Triumph and Disaster
  And treat those two impostors just the same;
If you can bear to hear the truth you've spoken
  Twisted by knaves to make a trap for fools,
Or watch the things you gave your life to, broken,
  And stoop and build 'em up with worn-out tools:

If you can make one heap of all your winnings
  And risk it on one turn of pitch-and-toss,
And lose, and start again at your beginnings
  And never breathe a word about your loss;
If you can force your heart and nerve and sinew
  To serve your turn long after they are gone,
And so hold on when there is nothing in you
  Except the Will which says to them: "Hold on!"

If you can talk with crowds and keep your virtue,
  Or walk with Kings - nor lose the common touch,
if neither foes nor loving friends can hurt you,
  If all men count with you, but none too much;
If you can fill the unforgiving minute
  With sixty seconds' worth of distance run,
Yours is the Earth and everything that's in it,
  And - which is more - you'll be a Man, my son!

The Sons of the Widow

'Ave you 'eard o' the Widow at Windsor
   With a hairy gold crown on 'er 'ead?
She 'as ships on the foam -- she 'as millions at 'ome,
    An' she pays us poor beggars in red.
      (Ow, poor beggars in red!)

There's 'er nick on the cavalry 'orses,
   There's 'er mark on the medical stores --
An' 'er troopers you'll find with a fair wind be'ind
    That takes us to various wars.
      (Poor beggars! -- barbarious wars!)

Then 'ere's to the Widow at Windsor,
   An' 'ere's to the stores an' the guns,
The men an' the 'orses what makes up the forces
    O' Missis Victorier's sons.
      (Poor beggars! Victorier's sons!)

Walk wide o' the Widow at Windsor,
   For 'alf o' Creation she owns:
We 'ave bought 'er the same with the sword an' the flame,
    An' we've salted it down with our bones.
      (Poor beggars! -- it's blue with our bones!)

Hands off o' the sons o' the Widow,
   Hands off o' the goods in 'er shop,
For the Kings must come down an' the Emperors frown
    When the Widow at Windsor says "Stop"!
      (Poor beggars! -- we're sent to say "Stop"!)

Then 'ere's to the Lodge o' the Widow,
   From the Pole to the Tropics it runs --
To the Lodge that we tile with the rank an' the file,
    An' open in form with the guns.
      (Poor beggars! -- it's always they guns!)

We 'ave 'eard o' the Widow at Windsor,
    It's safest to let 'er alone:
For 'er sentries we stand by the sea an' the land
    Wherever the bugles are blown.
        (Poor beggars! -- an' don't we get blown!)

Take 'old o' the Wings o' the Mornin',
    An' flop round the earth till you're dead;
But you won't get away from the tune that they play
    To the bloomin' old rag over'ead.
        (Poor beggars! -- it's 'ot over'ead!)

Then 'ere's to the sons o' the Widow,
    Wherever, 'owever they roam.
'Ere's all they desire, an' if they require
    A speedy return to their 'ome.
        (Poor beggars! -- they'll never see 'ome!)

Banquet Night

'Once in so often,' King Solomon said,
    Watching his quarrymen drill the stone,
'We will club our garlic and wine and bread
    And banquet together beneath my Throne
And all the Brethren shall come to that mess
As Fellow-Craftsmen—no more and no less.

'Send a swift shallop to Hiram of Tyre,
    Felling and floating our beautiful trees,
Say that the Brethren and I desire
    Talk with our Brethren who use the seas.
And we shall be happy to meet them at mess
As Fellow-Craftsmen—no more and no less.

'Carry this message to Hiram Abif—
    Excellent Master of forge and mine:—
I and the Brethren would like it if
    He and the Brethren will come to dine
(Garments from Bozrah or morning-dress)
As Fellow-Craftsmen—no more and no less.

'God gave the Hyssop and Cedar their place—
    Also the Bramble, the Fig and the Thorn—
But that is no reason to black a man's face
    Because he is not what he hasn't been born.
And, as touching the Temple, I hold and profess
We are Fellow-Craftsmen—no more and no less.'

So it was ordered and so it was done,
    And the hewers of wood and the Masons of Mark,
With foc'sle hands of the Sidon run
    And Navy Lords from the *Royal Ark*,
Came and sat down and were merry at mess
As Fellow-Craftsmen—no more and no less.

The Quarries are hotter than Hiram's forge,
    No one is safe from the dog-whips' reach.

It's mostly snowing up Lebanon gorge,
    And it's always blowing off Joppa beach;

But once in so often, the messenger brings
Solomon's mandate: 'Forget these things!
Brother to Beggars and Fellow to Kings,
Companion of Princes—forget these things!
Fellow-Craftsman, forget these things!'

The Palace

When I was a King and a Mason - a Master proven and skilled
I cleared me ground for a Palace such as a King should build.
I decreed and dug down to my levels. Presently under the silt
I came on the wreck of a Palace such as a King had built.

There was no worth in the fashion - there was no wit in the plan -
Hither and thither, aimless, the ruined footings ran -
Masonry, brute, mishandled, but carven on every stone:
"After me cometh a Builder. Tell him I too have known."

Swift to my use in the trenches, where my well-planned ground-works grew,
I tumbled his quoins and his ashlars, and cut and reset them anew.
Lime I milled of his marbles; burned it slacked it, and spread;
Taking and leaving at pleasure the gifts of the humble dead.

Yet I despised not nor gloried; yet, as we wrenched them apart,
I read in the razed foundations the heart of that builder's heart.
As he had written and pleaded, so did I understand
The form of the dream he had followed in the face of the thing he had
planned.

*   *   *

When I was a King and a Mason, in the open noon of my pride,
They sent me a Word from the Darkness. They whispered and called me aside.
They said - "The end is forbidden." They said - "Thy use is fulfilled.
"Thy Palace shall stand as that other's - the spoil of a King who shall build."

I called my men from my trenches, my quarries my wharves and my sheers.
All I had wrought I abandoned to the faith of the faithless years.
Only I cut on the timber - only I carved on the stone:
"After me cometh a Builder. Tell him, I too have known!"

The Thousandth Man

One man in a thousand, Solomon says,
    Will stick more close than a brother.
And it's worth while seeking him half your days
    If you find him before the other.
Nine hundred and ninety-nine depend
    On what the world sees in you,
But the Thousandth man will stand your friend
    With the whole round world agin' you.

'Tis neither promise nor prayer nor show
    Will settle the finding for 'ee.
Nine hundred and ninety-nine of 'em go
    By your looks, or your acts, or your glory.
But if he finds you and you find him.
    The rest of the world don't matter;
For the Thousandth Man will sink or swim
    With you in any water.

You can use his purse with no more talk
    Than he uses yours for his spendings,
And laugh and meet in your daily walk
    As though there had been no lendings.
Nine hundred and ninety-nine of 'em call
    For silver and gold in their dealings;
But the Thousandth Man he's worth 'em all,
    Because you can show him your feelings.

His wrong's your wrong, and his right's your right,
    In season or out of season.
Stand up and back it in all men's sight —
    With that for your only reason!
Nine hundred and ninety-nine can't bide
    The shame or mocking or laughter,
But the Thousandth Man will stand by your side
    To the gallows-foot — and after!

A Pilgrim's Way

I do not look for holy saints to guide me on my way
Or male and female devilkins to lead my feet astray.
If these are added I rejoice - if not, I shall not mind
So long as I have leave and choice to meet my fellow-kind.
    For as we come and as we go (and deadly soon go we!)
    The people, lord, Thy people, are good enough for me.

Thus I will honour pious men whose virtue shines so bright
(Though none are more amazed than I when I by chance do right)
And I will pity foolish men for woe their sins have bred
(Though ninety-nine percent of mine I brought on my own head)
    And Amorite or Eremite or General Averagee
    The people, Lord, Thy people are good enough for me

And when the bore me overmuch, I will not shake mine ears
Recalling many thousand such whom I have bored to tears
And when they labour to impress I will not doubt nor scoff
Since I myself have done no less and sometimes pulled it off
    Yea as we are and we are not and we pretend to be
    The people, lord, Thy people, are good enough for me.

And when they work me random wrong as oftentimes hath been
I will not cherish hate too long (my hands are none too clean)
And when they do me random good I will not feign surprise
No more than those whom I have cheered with wayside courtesies
    But as we give and as we take - whate'er our takings be)
    The people, lord, Thy people, are good enough for me.

But when I meet with frantic folk who sinfully declare
There is no pardon for their sin, the same I will not spare
Till I have proved that Heaven and Hell which in our hearts we have
Show nothing irredeemable on either side the grave
    For as we live and as we die - if utter Death there be
    The people, lord, Thy people, are good enough for me.

Deliver me from every pride - the Middle, High and Low

That bars me from a brother's side, whatever pride he show
And purge me from all heresies of thought and speech and pen
That bid me judge him otherwise than I am judged. Amen
That I might sing of Crowd or King or road-borne company
That I may labour in my day, vocation and degree
To prove the same by deed and name, and hold unshakenly
(Where'er I go, whate'er I know, whoe'er my neighbour be)
    This single faith in Life and Death and to Eternity
    "The people, lord, Thy people, are good enough for me."

My New-cut Ashlar

My new-cut ashlar takes the light
   Where crimson-blank the windows flare
By my own work before the night,
   Great Overseer, I make my prayer.

If there be good in that I wrought
   Thy Hand compelled it, Master, Thine -
Where I have failed to meet Thy Thought
   I know, through Thee, the blame was mine.

One instant's toil to Thee denied
   Stands all Eternity's offence.
Of that I did with Thee to guide,
   To Thee, through Thee, be excellence.

The depth and dream of my desire,
   The bitter paths wherein I stray -
Thou knowest Who hast made the Fire,
   Thou knowest Who hast made the Clay.

Who, lest all thought of Eden fade,
   Bring'st Eden to the craftsman's brain -
Godlike to muse o'er his own Trade
   And manlike stand with God again!

One stone the more swings into place
   In that dread Temple of Thy worth.
It is enough that, through Thy Grace.
   I saw nought common on Thy Earth.

Take not that vision from my ken -
   Oh whatsoe'er may spoil or speed.
Help me to need no aid from men
   That I may help such men as need!

www.ingramcontent.com/pod-product-compliance
Lightning Source LLC
Chambersburg PA
CBHW020343260626
47156CB00004B/1673